TESTIMONY OF INNOCENCE

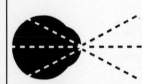

This Large Print Book carries the
Seal of Approval of N.A.V.H.

TESTIMONY OF INNOCENCE

DEBORAH LYNNE

THORNDIKE PRESS
A part of Gale, Cengage Learning

GALE
CENGAGE Learning·

Farmington Hills, Mich • San Francisco • New York • Waterville, Maine
Meriden, Conn • Mason, Ohio • Chicago

GALE
CENGAGE Learning®

LIBRARY OF CONGRESS CATALOGING-IN-PUBLICATION DATA

Lynne, Deborah, 1953–
    Testimony of innocence / by Deborah Lynne. — Large print edition.
        pages cm. — (The bayou secrets romance ; 3) (Thorndike Press large print clean reads)
        ISBN 978-1-4104-8094-1 (hardcover) — ISBN 1-4104-8094-1 (hardcover)
        1. Large type books. I. Title.
    PS3612.Y5517T47 2015
    813'.6—dc23   2015017997

Published in 2015 by arrangement with Barbour Publishing, Inc.

Printed in Mexico
1 2 3 4 5 6 7 19 18 17 16 15

I dedicate this book to
my critique partners, Emy and Marie,
who have believed in me
for a very long time.
Thank you for your encouragement
along the way.

And, as always, God and my family.
Without them, I am nothing.

ACKNOWLEDGMENTS

The Samantha Cain series has been a dream of mine for almost twenty years. If it wasn't for my friends and family who believe in me, it would probably still be a dream. I look forward to many books to follow and hope everyone enjoys them!

Charlotte and Marty, thanks for your help in the final stages of *Testimony of Innocence.*

Emy and Marie, I can never thank you enough for your love, support, and critiquing, but I'll keep trying.

Ramona Tucker, my editor, thanks for believing in me. You're the best editor anyone could ask for, and you really live your faith. I'm proud to be part of the family at OakTara.

Last, but not least, I thank You, Lord, for calling me to write fiction and for giving me the ability to share Your love in every one of my books.

"I have told you these things,
so that in me you may have peace.
In this world you will have trouble.
But take heart! I have overcome the world."

JOHN 16:33 NIV

CHAPTER 1

Three hard knocks sounded on the front door, awakening Samantha from her short nap on the couch after working the night shift.

She stirred. *Open your eyes.*

Forcing her eyes open, Samantha glanced at her watch.

Umph. Nearly time for her to wake her son, Marty, for school.

Three more raps pounded on the door.

Who could that be at this early hour?

Instantly, an image from six short months ago flashed through her mind. Two police officers stood at her apartment door with bad news: Matthew Jefferies, her fiancé, had been killed in the line of duty.

Her insides coiled as she rose. Ice tipped her fingers as she stared at the door, her feet frozen to the floor.

The demanding knocks came a third time. Against her better judgment, she moved in the direction of the front door. Taking a cleansing, reassuring breath, she slowly reached out for the doorknob. The cold round ball matched the chill within. Only bad news came this early in the morning. "Give me that extra strength, Lord," she whispered.

A single thought allowed her a moment of cheer. Maybe Greg, Matthew's dear friend and now hers, or Amanda, her best friend for many years, decided to drop by to say hello and check on her and Marty. But that pleasing idea vanished almost as fast as it had come. She knew better. Emptiness gnawed at her heart as she released the breath she'd held and forced herself to open the door.

Morning light spilled inside the door, revealing two strange men standing on the front porch. Both were dressed in off-the-rack suits: one brown, one blue. Glancing behind the unexpected men, she saw a dark blue government-issued car parked in the driveway and realized the men were plain-clothed police officers, detectives of some sort. This reality intensified the grip on her insides as she tightened her hold on the doorknob.

Not again. She bit her bottom lip, trying to retain control of her emotions. What could they possibly want with her?

"Hello. May I help you?" Her tone surprised her. It sounded calm, almost peaceful, as if she were glad to find them standing on her front steps.

But voices, she knew, could be deceiving. In her heart, she wanted to yell at them to go away. It had only been six months since Matthew died — a week before their wedding. You'd think after that tragedy she could handle anything that came her way. But she was still grieving.

"Samantha Cain?" The man in the brown suit flashed his badge.

"Yes."

"I'm Lieutenant Jones, and this is Sergeant Barnett. May we come in?"

As the first man spoke, the man in blue also exposed his badge, as if making sure there was no misunderstanding that both were police detectives, there on official business.

She opened the door wider. "Please come in. Take a seat. I'll be back in a minute. I have to wake my son for school."

Shivers raced through her as she walked out of the living room. She wanted to run and hide. What was this about? Her heart tightened.

At least her son — the most important

11

thing in her life — was fine. She planned to keep him safe and guard him from the ugliness of the world. In the first eight years of his life, Marty had already lived through too much. First, his father, who took his own life, and then the death of Matthew, who planned to be his future father — truly his daddy.

What more could possibly go wrong?

Sam also knew her parents were fine. She had spoken to them last night.

What else was there?

Who else was there?

She sighed. Whatever it was, she would handle it. Life would still go on, day after day.

Knocking on Marty's door, she stepped into the room and slipped over to his bedside. "Hey, baby, it's time to get up. Get ready for school," she whispered, shaking him gently. "Rise and shine." She stepped to the window and rolled the plastic pole slightly with her fingertips, opening the blinds a crack. Sunlight spilled into his room.

"Aw, Mom, do I have to?" His little body stretched as he tried to open his eyes. Twisting under his covers, he hid his face from the light and tried to go back to sleep.

The boy knew the answer before he asked,

so she didn't bother to respond. He would get up. That she also knew. He loved school — the learning and the playing.

"We have company, so I may not get to make you breakfast," she told him in a matter-of-fact tone. "You can fix yourself a bowl of cereal, or better still, tap on Ms. Margaret's door. Tell her I have some company and ask her if she'll fix you something this morning. Tell her I'll explain later. Right now, I'll go put on the coffee pot for her." She ruffled her son's dark reddish hair. "Get up now. Be a good boy."

Taking another route back to the living room, she slipped through the kitchen and turned on the coffeemaker. Margaret always pre-cleaned and set the machine with grounds and water the night before. The woman was such a blessing in Sam's life.

Next Sam walked through the swinging door separating the kitchen from the living room. The floor plan of Matthew's home, now hers and Marty's home, was laid out exceptionally well. The house was warm, cozy, efficient.

Matthew had listed Samantha as his beneficiary, leaving everything to her, including his house. At first it had been strange and unsettling living there without him in it, especially since that was where they had planned to live once married. After a short time she realized the blessing. Living there now kept his image, his scent, her memories of him, and the time they'd spent together closer to her and to Marty. Matthew had been a strong influence in her son's life, even though the time had been short. Already his home felt like theirs, with only great memories hidden in the shadows.

"Now, gentlemen, what can I do for you?" Masking her insecurities, she perched on Matthew's favorite chair across from them. Matthew may not be there for her now, but she felt his presence in his things.

"We have a few questions for you," the lieutenant said as Sergeant Barnett pulled out a pad and pen.

"About what? What questions could you possibly have for me? You two are detectives, right? From which precinct and which division?" As a former cop's wife, Sam knew there were several divisions, such as robbery, homicide, burglary, and even a general investigations division. But she had no idea what they could possibly want with her.

"When was the last time you saw your boss, Ken Richardson? And what did you two talk about?"

"My boss?" Them asking questions about Ken had never entered her mind. She had to think on that one — for two reasons. One, she didn't get along that well with her boss and tried to keep her distance from him as much as possible; and two, she worked the night shift, which gave her little, if any, contact with him. He left every day at four thirty on the dot, and she worked the night shift, 6:00 p.m. to 6:00 a.m.

"Is Ken okay?" For the two of them to come to her door, something had to have happened to Ken. But still, why come to her? She only worked for the man. Sam only knew him as a boss.

"Answer our questions, Ms. Cain. When was the last time you saw or spoke with Ken Richardson?"

"I don't understand why you'd be asking me about my boss. What's wrong? Did he do something wrong or did something happen to him? No one mentioned anything about him last night at work when I went on duty. And no one called about him during the night. I was there all night. So why are you asking me about my boss this early in the morning?"

Sam hoped he was okay. Even though she didn't get along very well with the man, she didn't want to see anything bad happen to him. As a person, a family man, he was great . . . just not as a boss.

"Ms. Cain, please. Answer the questions. We can bring you in to the station if you'd rather answer our questions there."

She pulled in a quick breath. *Bring me down to the station?* Shivers slid across her shoulders. Sam didn't want to go there. *This is ridiculous. Why ask me about Ken? They should talk to Dorothy.*

"Again, when was the last time you saw your boss?"

She shrugged. "I'm not sure. The last dispatch meeting we had, I guess. And that was over a month ago."

"You guess?" Jones questioned, his brows raised, his eyes burning a hole through her. Then a smug look crossed his features. "Why are you asking if he's okay? What do you know about him?"

"I don't know anything. I'm asking because you're asking me questions about him. And you came to my house to do it. That tells me something is wrong. So what happened? Where is he? Is he okay?"

"Please, Ms. Cain. You need to answer my questions." His growl shook her to the core. "You said the last time you saw him was at a dispatch meeting, but then you said *you guess.* Did you or did you not last see him at that meeting?"

"You misunderstand. I'm sure I saw him

16

at the last dispatcher's meeting. He runs them, and I was there. I just can't be sure if I've seen him *since* the meeting. I don't see him very much since I work nights. He's gone before I come on duty. The only time I see him is when we have a dispatcher's meeting, or when he calls me in for a private meeting — to question me on how I handled a particular incident. I don't think that's happened since the last dispatcher meeting . . . but I'm not positive. Give me a second." Squinting, she glanced from one man to the other.

As much as she tried to concentrate on the last time she saw Ken, the fact the detectives were at her house talking to her about him would not let go of her brain. Finally she said, "I still don't understand why you are asking *me* questions about Ken, unless something has happened to him. And then, still, why ask me? I don't know the man outside of work." She shook her head. "Something's got to be wrong. Please tell me he's okay?"

Ignoring her plea, Sergeant Barnett wrote as the lieutenant continued his interrogation. "Where were you last night between midnight and 4:00 a.m.?"

She rolled her eyes. *Do they not listen when I speak? Didn't I tell him I was there all night?*

17

Keep your cool. Drawing a relaxing breath, she took a second to control her tone. "At work, like I said. I work the night shift, six at night to six in the morning, four nights a week. Sunday nights through Thursday mornings."

What was going on? No hints, no clues were given so she asked again, "Why are you here? Is Ken okay? Please tell me at least that much." Her nerves tightened like strings on a guitar as the tuning pegs are twisted. Why couldn't they answer her questions? She answered theirs.

"We'll get to that, ma'am. Did you talk to Mr. Richardson last night from work? Did you call him? Or did he call you?"

Something doesn't feel right. Uneasiness crept through her. *Maybe Ken got arrested for something.*

"Has he done something wrong? Something illegal? At least tell me that." Tired of this one-sided conversation, Sam tried to stand her ground. "I want to know what's going on before I say anything else to you — not that I like the guy or anything, and I'm not out to protect him, but I don't want to be the one accused of getting him in trouble either." She had to look out for herself. Since she worked for the man, she was the one who would have to put up with any repercussions from this interrogation. No one else would protect her — not anymore.

Besides, she knew if she got Richardson in trouble, there would be payback later . . . although she had to admit he had been nicer to her since her engagement to Matthew. Even since Matthew's death, Ken had remained a decent guy to her, and she for one would like to keep it that way.

A frown creased Barnett's forehead as he glanced at Lieutenant Jones.

"Please, ma'am," Jones said, even though the tone didn't say *please,* "we need the answers to these questions. If you don't want to answer them here, like I said before, we can take you down to headquarters."

"This is absurd." She shifted, straightening her spine. She hadn't been to the station since the day after Matthew's funeral. They had brought her in to give her his belongings from his desk, things they had cleared out. Other than that, she had handled all her dealings with the police station through the lawyer Matthew had used when he drew up his will. That was more contact than she cared to have with the police station . . . then, now, or ever.

Her insides quivered at the thought of going back down there. *No.* She wasn't ready.

Blinking her eyes rapidly, she held back the tears that threatened as memories washed over her like a sudden downpour of rain. Her shoulders sagged. "Okay. What was the question again?"

"Did you talk to Ken Richardson last night while you were at work?"

Keeping her voice steady, she replied, "As I said earlier, no one talked to me about him, nor did I talk to Ken last night."

"You didn't call him from work around midnight last night?"

"No. Most definitely not." Lifting both her hands, palms out as if giving up, she waved them vigorously. "Trust me." Then thrusting her thumb toward her chest, she said, "I would have remembered if I'd called and had to wake him up at that time of night. He likes us to handle all situations. We only call him in extreme emergencies."

"And he didn't come by the office during the night?"

"No," she said decisively.

Barnett's gaze jumped from Samantha Cain back to his partner.

Jones eyed her suspiciously. "Did anything strange happen at your place of business last night?"

Sam dragged her fingers through her long brown hair, still in disarray from her short nap. She restrained from the desire to pull her hair out; they were driving her so crazy. *I have rights . . . don't I?*

Locking her gaze on the lieutenant, she lifted her chin boldly. "Look, I demand you tell me what this is all about. I have a right to know. I've answered your questions. At least let me know he's okay." She folded her arms across her chest, ready to keep her mouth shut and say no more, even if it meant going down to the station.

If he was in trouble, that was one thing, but if something happened to him, she wanted to know. Dorothy, his wife, may need someone to talk to. The woman had been there for her when Matthew died. Sam wanted to be there for Dorothy, if needed.

Apparently they got the message, because the lieutenant glared straight into her eyes and said, "Your boss was found dead on the floor of his office this morning."

CHAPTER 2

A gasp escaped Samantha Cain's lips as she jumped to her feet. "What?" Her eyes opened wide with real shock. "Ken, dead?"

She wasn't acting; Mark Barnett sensed it in his gut. The woman didn't know her boss was dead. Her head shook, as if not wanting to believe this had happened nor understanding how this could have happened. Blood drained from her face. Her strength seemed to suddenly slip away as her knees wobbled and her body drifted slowly toward the floor. The sergeant leapt to his feet and grabbed her by the elbow, trying to steady her.

Samantha yanked loose from his hold and held on to the nearby chair arm with a vise-like grip, her knuckles turning white. After a moment, she settled into the seat. "How could this be?" she asked almost in a whisper, but it didn't sound like a question directed to the detectives.

"Are you all right?" Mark asked, trying to keep his tone business-as-usual but wanting to offer support in her time of distress. Jones might not care, but Mark had known Detective Jefferies and how much he loved this woman. He could see the appeal — strong yet fragile, plain and simple yet beautiful. And that long, straight, silky brown hair that fell around her shoulders . . . what's not to like? He had heard rumors of her first marriage and the tragic ending, and then the poor woman went through the death of her fiancé. Samantha Cain deserved a little respect and sympathy in his opinion. He didn't want to put Detective Matthew's fiancée through this torment. She didn't deserve it.

But his superior seemed to enjoy the misery he was putting her through.

"This can't be," she whispered. "Ken, dead?" Doubt filled her eyes. "He can't be dead. I don't believe it." Suddenly the cloudiness in her eyes vanished. Turning her gaze first on Jones and then on Barnett, she asked, "How? And you said he was found upstairs? In his office? This morning?" Slowly she leaned back into the chair. "That couldn't be. I never saw him last night."

"Okay. So you were there last night, well, early this morning. Did you hear or see anything?" Mark tried to encourage her to think and give an answer that would throw suspicion off of her.

Jones probably didn't like his question, but Mark didn't care. He had to give the woman a chance. Wasn't it innocent until proven guilty? They were supposed to ask questions to see if she heard or saw anything, not questions trying to incriminate her. Mark eased back down on the sofa and picked up his pad and pen again, ready to write should she respond. He regretted his swift glance at the lieutenant's face. No doubt Jones would give him grief when they got in the car. Oh well. Mark would deal with it then.

Staring but seeing nothing, Sam rubbed her temples. Reality started sinking in. This had to be a bad dream. Who would kill Ken? Well, he had plenty of enemies, but to kill him and be found dead at work? While she was at work, no less!

"I can't believe it. I just can't believe it," she mumbled over and over to herself. Pivoting toward the detectives, she looked straight into Jones' eyes. "Ken wasn't there last night. He would have come into my office and spoken to me had he been there. So how could he be found dead in his office this morning? It makes no sense." Confusion and disgust filled her with frustration.

I'd know if he'd come in last night. I would have seen him enter the front door. Surely he'd have said hello and then gone up to his office. Why sneak in the back way and not reveal his presence to me? And be dead? Who? How?

To the detectives she had stated it like fact that the man never came to the job last night, but then in her brain she had to convince herself of those same words. In truth, she wondered, would he have spoken to her? He barely did whenever they came face-to-face. But why not at least make his presence known to her?

So how did he end up upstairs this morning . . . dead?

Closing her eyes, she frantically tried to recall anything strange — a sound, footsteps, a large thump in the night — that might suggest he was upstairs in his office while she worked downstairs. Admittedly, he could have slipped up the back way without telling her, but why would he? It made no sense . . . unless he was hiding something . . . or someone? Someone he didn't want her to know was there with him.

That thought confused her even more. He wouldn't do that to Dorothy. Would he? But neither did it make sense that Ken was dead. She blew out a rush of air.

Lieutenant Jones threw the next question at her, and it hit her like a sucker punch in the gut. "You were the only one at your place of business last night, right?"

"Yes. At times. I mean, the guys in the back worked until 11:30. That's two mechanics and a rack-man. After that, a few of the drivers came in to leave out on a run. That was from about 3:00 a.m. on through the morning. Other than that, I thought I was there by myself." Her teeth scraped her bottom lip as her mind whirled in wonder.

How could I not have heard him upstairs moving around? A man that size couldn't be too quiet, could he?

"So from 11:30 p.m. until 3:00 a.m. you were alone?" Jones' question sounded more convicting than questioning.

She clasped her fingers together while thinking hard. "I thought so, but apparently I wasn't." Dropping her hands to her sides, her fingers formed tight fists as the lieutenant's expression told her he'd found the guilty party.

Then she remembered. "Wait," she said, pointing her finger in the air. "I also had a driver come in around 2:00 or 2:30, but he was coming in off the road to go home.

26

Maybe he saw something." She grabbed onto the hope.

"We'll need his name, as well as the others who were coming and going," the sergeant stated, sounding almost gentle. "You're right. They may have seen something."

Sam couldn't help but glance his way. With the way the lieutenant was questioning her, her heart longed for someone to believe in her. She gave him a tight-lipped smile, hoping it reached her eyes. That was her way of saying, "Thanks for sounding like you believe in me." He didn't seem to be accusing her like Jones was. Relief slid through her veins as some of the tension slipped away from her shoulders and neck.

"Sure. No problem. Maybe one of them saw something." She hoped, anyway. Sam studied the lieutenant, trying to read his thoughts, hoping they would reflect Barnett's words.

Oh well. One maybe believing her was better than no one believing her.

Returning her gaze to Sergeant Barnett, she asked, "What happened to him? I mean, how did he . . . die? When did he die?"

Could she have saved him? She wondered. Sam covered her mouth with her hands and then gently slid her fingers away as these questions hit her full force. Swallowing the hard lump that had formed in her throat, she whispered, "Sorry."

She hadn't even seen Ken come to the yard and go upstairs, let alone to the building — or anyone else for that matter. Sam couldn't recall any cars driving in during the night. Of course her back was to the entrance when she worked logs, and when she keyed things into the computer updating the loads and deliveries. Sam always used the computer facing the drivers' window so she would know when someone was standing there, waiting for her help. She rarely paid attention to traffic out on the highway, even at midnight or 1:00 in the morning, for that matter. Over the years she'd learned to ignore outside intrusions. Usually it was a driver coming in to go out, or someone dropping him off. Occasionally, it was a drunk and he'd lost his way. But even those interruptions didn't disturb her anymore.

The last time anything bad had happened was a little over a year ago, when a serial killer had strangled a poor woman and Sam had tried to save her.

Truth hit her. Of course she couldn't have saved him. If she couldn't save that little woman last year, how in the world could she possibly think she could have saved her boss, a big man of six-foot-six? Anyone hurting him had to be as big, if not bigger.

"We don't have the coroner's report yet," Jones cut in before Barnett could answer, "so we're not sure of any specific details at the moment. I have a few more questions for you, though. Other than drivers and the men who were working with you till 11:30, did you see anyone else enter the parking lot or the building?"

"No stranger, if that's what you mean. Besides, Ken Richardson wasn't even there last night. I would have seen him, I tell you. He would have said something to me had he come by there last night. I'm sure of it."

Sometimes Mother Nature called, she reminded herself but didn't share that with them. Surely they knew no one could watch twelve hours straight for intruders while performing their work duties without some sort of break.

Hoping to explain things a little better, she added, "It's the same routine every night — well, Monday night through Friday morning. He leaves before I get there; locks his office upstairs before he goes. The only one having a key to get in his office besides him is the shop foreman. I never see my boss. And I surely don't understand why

29

someone would want to kill him. Sure, there are times I wish he wasn't around, but I would never kill him."

Jones watched Sam intently. His eyes sparkled with delight, as if she had made a full confession.

Sergeant Barnett said quickly, "We didn't accuse you, ma'am. We're merely asking you questions."

"I know. I didn't think you were." She didn't, but now she wasn't so sure.

The way the lieutenant had perked up and then the way the sergeant jumped on that statement made her think that maybe they *were* accusing her. She wondered if earlier she had only wished someone believed in her. Now she questioned her hope in Barnett for believing in her. She'd noted the lieutenant had watched her reaction with a keen eye, but that she expected. He was a cop. But the way Sergeant Barnett stated so swiftly they weren't accusing her, though, alerted her senses. She had seen enough crime shows on television to know police don't always mean what they say.

Second thoughts made her wonder. As kind as the sergeant seemed only moments ago, maybe he wasn't condemning her but warning her to watch how she spoke. She had better watch her step and keep a tight lid on what she said. She might be a suspect in Ken's death after all. Oh, how she wished Matthew was here with her to counsel her, to protect her.

Obviously they asked her questions for a reason. "Questions for a person of interest," Matthew used to call them. Maybe these two truly thought she did it, since she was the only one there most of the night. But really, truly, would she be that dumb? Would anyone kill him at the office where he or she would be the only suspect? Not to mention she'd never kill him . . . or anyone else . . . for that matter.

She nearly laughed to herself. At six-foot-six, Ken had weighed close to 300 pounds. She was a mere half an inch taller than five feet, weighing 140 pounds. He would squash her like a bug. In fact, her boss used his size to intimidate her and others — and it worked most of the time.

Since Sam had been engaged to Matthew, Ken hadn't antagonized her as much. And since Matthew's death, Ken continued to keep his distance from Sam. She guessed in the beginning it was because Matthew was a police detective. Richardson probably figured out the law might be on her side. Smart thinking on his part. Or, after Matthew's death, it could have been out of respect to the dead that he never returned to his old ways of torture.

"So do you have any more questions, or are we through? I need to get my son off to school so he won't be late."

"Are you sure you didn't call him last night around midnight?" Jones blurted.

"Positive. Anything else?" She was ready for them to leave.

"Not at this time, Ms. Cain, but we need a list of names from you of everyone you remember passing through the terminal last night, including the men who worked in the shop." Jones' voice seemed cold, and his smugness made her antsy. "And who did you say had the other key to his office?"

"Our shop foreman. Otto Thomas."

As she began to give the names of the drivers and workers who had passed through or worked during the night, Barnett flipped his paper over, giving himself a clean sheet to write on.

After Sam named everyone she could remember, she said, "You can call the office, too. I'm sure they will give you these guys' cell numbers or addresses so you can reach them for questioning also."

When finished writing the names given, the sergeant smiled slightly and thanked her for her time.

"We'll be in touch," Jones said sharply. On those words they left.

After shutting the front door, Sam's first reaction, besides shaking all over, was to call Greg.

Greg Singleton was Matthew's father's partner years ago and a dear friend to Matthew. Greg had come back into Matthew's life when he was working on catching the serial killer that roamed the Baton Rouge area last year. As Matthew and Sam's relationship grew, so did a friendship between her and Greg. After Matthew's passing, Greg had been there for them, and now she considered him to be her and Marty's friend for life. The man had retired from the force a few years back and now worked as a special agent assigned to protect the governor.

Clutching the phone, she punched out his phone number and then pressed it against her ear, listening as it rang.

After two rings she heard Greg's voice say, "Hello. You've reached 555-1418. I can't come to the phone right now, but if you'll leave your name and number, I'll get back to you as soon as possible."

She hated speaking to machines, but at the moment she was glad he had one. "Greg, it's me. My boss is dead, and I think the police think I had something to do with it. Please call me right away." Desperation resonated in her voice. She couldn't control it. A tight-fisted grip snagged her heart.

Dropping the phone into the cradle, she knew Greg would get back to her right away — as soon as he heard the message anyway. She just prayed it was in time.

A sigh slipped through her lips. Now to tell Margaret without alerting Marty to the fact that anything was wrong.

CHAPTER 3

Slipping on a smile to mask the lines of stress, Sam strode toward the swinging door to the kitchen. Marty was a smart kid. He'd be full of questions. And Margaret? She'd read the concern in Sam's eyes in no time. So Sam did her best to conceal her eyes by lowering her head as she entered. "Good morning, everyone. Thanks for filling in this morning for me, Margaret."

Marty's back was to her, but Margaret locked eyes with Sam over Marty's head. In one instant, the wise woman clearly saw through the lowered lashes. Margaret's hazel eyes told Sam she'd kept Marty busy, but as soon as he was off to school, she wanted all the details.

Glancing back at her son, Sam saw he was drinking the last of the milk in his cereal bowl. "Okay, Marty. Go brush your teeth. It's time for school."

"Who were those guys, Mom?" He put

down his dish and turned curious eyes her way. "What did they want, and why did they come so early?"

"Nothing concerning you, big boy. Now go get ready." She flashed him a smile with raised brows, hopefully conveying she meant business.

He grumbled but jumped down from his chair and hustled out of the kitchen.

Margaret rose and stepped next to Sam. "Okay. You sit and tell me quickly. I'll fix your coffee. Who was that at the door this early in the morning? And what did they want? I know it doesn't concern me either, but tell me what you can so I can be here for you." Margaret squeezed Sam's hand. "Really. Sit. I'll get you a cup of coffee."

Appreciating her friend, Sam did as she was told. She sat at the table, clasped her hands, and leaned forward. Her insides were a jumbled wreck. She didn't understand what was going on . . . and couldn't believe what she had been told. What happened to Ken? How did he die? And how did he end up at the office without her knowing? She didn't want to share all of her concerns with Margaret. The woman was a dear and very helpful over the past six months. Every day she was becoming more like a friend, but Sam didn't want to burden her with

36

everything. "My boss was killed last night," she murmured.

Margaret's eyes widened. In slow motion, she set a cup of coffee in front of Sam. Still moving at a snail's pace, she returned to her seat. "Killed? How?"

"They found him this morning at my job site." Sam started wringing her hands. "The sad thing is, I think they think I had something to do with it. I'm waiting for Greg to call me now. So when he calls, if I'm asleep, please wake me."

Sympathy poured from Margaret's eyes as she reached across the table and covered Sam's twisting hands, helping them stop their movement and relax. "It will be okay, Ms. Sam. You know I'm here for you and Marty. I love you both like family already. Whatever you need, I'm here for you. And don't you worry. Mr. Greg will take care of you and this misunderstanding." Her eyes were steady as she spoke in confidence.

When Marty raced back into the kitchen with his backpack, Margaret released her hold.

"I'm ready, Mom. Let's go." The little boy who didn't want to wake up for school this morning was now replaced by a child excited for another day of learning . . . or was it the playing at recess that excited him so?

Sam smiled thankfully at Margaret and, turning in her chair, opened her arms to her son. "Okay, let's go." He rushed into her arms and hugged her tight before heading out the back door. Rising to her feet, she said to Margaret, "If only I had half that amount of energy." Laughing, she followed him out the back door and to the car.

Keep me strong, Lord. I think the madness in my life is about to start all over again.

That night, the buzz at the office was unbelievable. Sam wished she'd heard from Greg before she had come to work, but she hadn't. He must have been on a job that took him out of town. Those usually lasted a few days.

Sam rubbed her temples, trying to make the headache she'd had all day go away. Sleep barely touched her eyes today so she felt certain tonight was going to be a tough one — trying to stay wide awake and handle all that went on in a normal night. Hopefully, there would be no problems. Unfortunately, by the gossip around the shop and drivers' room, it didn't sound like it would be a normal night. Everyone had his two cents to add to the situation.

The main office had already sent a temporary fill-in boss to keep the terminal running smoothly. Did it really help? She doubted it. Each person had a different idea on how Ken died, and everyone wanted to talk about it. All of a sudden, every driver, every wash-rack hand, every mechanic was his best friend and knew all about his private life. Of course, all anyone really knew was that he loved his family and loved to fish. To hear the guys talk now, they each knew who would have wanted to kill Ken. Of course, each of their suspects had different reasons for wanting the man dead, and they all sounded like pretty solid motives. Some maybe even the police would follow up on . . . she hoped anyway. Sam had no idea where they were getting their information. Who was to say if any of it was really true?

The first thing she'd learned years ago working at a trucking company was that you couldn't believe everything you heard from a driver and only half of what you saw. Sure, most of the rumors held a grain of truth, but by the tenth person passing on the story, not much of that truth was still in there — but it made a wonderful tale to keep the tongues wagging.

It was strange working tonight, knowing

her boss was dead. Sam wanted to call Dorothy and tell her how sorry she was for her loss, but maybe Ken's wife wasn't ready to hear from the people at work yet. Sam would wait a couple of days. At the funeral, she would talk to her.

Yellow tape stretched across the bottom of the stairs leading to the boss's office, which left a constant reminder that something horrible had happened in the building. Not that anyone needed reminding with all the talk floating around. The doors leading up the stairs were closed and locked behind the tape; however, that wasn't unusual. Only the bright yellow reminder made things odd. Oh, and, of course, the policeman hanging around the drivers' room in front of the double doors. That added to the peculiarity of it all.

I wonder if he'll be here all night.

According to the gossip, there had been cops in and out of the building all day long. At that moment, Sam was glad she worked nights and not days. Out back she saw that the yellow tape stating *CRIME SCENE — DO NOT CROSS* also ran across the bottom of the stairs out in the shop. These steps led up to a storage facility as well as to the main entrance of Otto Thomas' office. Through there was another door leading to the boss's office. At the bottom stood another police-man on guard. Since Richardson and Thomas held the only keys that unlocked the door that separated the two offices, only they could unlock the door. Sam guessed they kept it locked, but she wasn't sure.

Back in the earlier days, when she was the secretary, that door was kept wide-open most of the time. Of course, it was a differ-ent boss and different shop foreman then. The only time she recalled it being closed was when a meeting was going on in either office — but that was over five years ago.

Richardson liked his privacy. The day he started working at their terminal was the first day that door stayed shut between the two offices.

By midnight, her brain was so tired of listening to all the scuttlebutt, she couldn't wait to get out of there. The foot traffic in the office died down as the hour grew late. Most everyone was home in bed by now or already rolling down the road in the direc-tion of his consignee, the point of delivery for his load.

Since Greg hadn't returned her call, she knew he had to be on duty with the governor. Otherwise he would have called Sam's cell number, even if he'd gotten back late. Under contractual obligation with the governor, he was not allowed to talk with friends and family during his time on the job. It usually lasted no more than a couple of days at a time. She felt sure she'd hear from him soon. If only he could listen to the message sooner, Sam believed he'd find a way to get in touch with her.

Truth be told, she hadn't listened to the news lately, so she had no idea what was going on with the governor. Greg could be out of town protecting him for a week right now, for all she knew. Sam hoped he'd call soon. His advice was much needed.

"Hey, Sam. Have you been fingerprinted yet?" Ronnie called from the drivers' window, snapping her out of her thoughts. He'd slipped in without her noticing, but again, that wasn't unusual.

Tonight of all nights, after what happened last night without her knowledge, she should have been paying closer attention. But a cop was standing at the bottom of the front stairs and another at the back stairs. Surely they'd be watching the comings and goings of everyone. She had other things to handle. Besides, Sam had a hard enough time concentrating on work with so little sleep.

Her office was kept separate from the drivers' room as well as the entrance to the building. The policeman standing guard at the bottom of the stairs inside would see someone immediately when they walked in the glass door to the trucking company. The separation of the dispatch office from the entranceway had been added several years ago when a fight broke out between one of the drivers and a dispatcher. The angry driver had leaped over the short wall that originally separated the two rooms. In a matter of moments, that driver yanked the dispatcher up from his chair and was choking the life out of him.

The full-sized wall added since then had a window cut into the middle with a shelf built on the dispatch side. The structure kept a distance between the two parties without cutting off communication altogether. A thick clear plastic window filled the area from top to bottom. An opening about ten inches across and four inches tall allowed paperwork to be passed from dispatcher to driver and vice-versa. Also a small hole, about the size of a fist, was cut into the middle of the window about five feet up from the ground. This allowed conversation between dispatcher and driver.

The terminal's front, back, and side doors were double locked, making it difficult to exit or enter the offices of the building. Safety loomed all around them, except when the night dispatcher had to unlock one of the doors to get a cold drink or snack from the machine in the drivers' room, to put logs in the drivers' boxes, or to walk out back to the lunchroom and heat up his or her dinner in the microwave. During this time, anyone who wanted to could slip in quietly and hide in the office to catch the dispatcher off guard later.

That scenario only occurred to Sam when she first started working nights and saw how dark and secluded the building and grounds were late at night. At that time, she locked the door behind her coming and going. In a short time, she got past her moments of concern and rarely locked the back door when going to heat up her dinner. The extra time spent on putting her dinner down to lock or unlock the door, along with the fact that the phone would sometimes ring at just that moment, caused her to eventually quit locking it behind her most nights. Sam's faith was in a mighty God who took care of her. She only had to learn to listen to Him closely. He urged her at the right times when to lock the door.

"No, I sure haven't been fingerprinted. Why?" As she asked Ronnie, her mind wondered for a moment why her prints weren't taken. And then as quickly she remembered that last year her prints had gone into the system during the time the police were trying to solve the killing across the highway. The killing she had tried to prevent but failed. The police didn't need to take them again she thought as she added, "Have you?" She reached for his packet of paperwork that was held in a wall file with all the rest of the packets for loads sitting on the yard, waiting to be delivered.

Ronnie was a driver she considered to be a friend. They had both worked for the company for about the same length of time, and there was almost as much love lost between him and the boss as there was between Sam and the boss — even though she didn't like the fact someone had killed Ken. In fact, not too many workers cared for Ken Richardson, although several took credit earlier in their gossip session for being one of his best buddies.

"Yeah. They caught me this morning before I headed out to go load. In fact, they said they were requesting all employees' prints. Like we really had a choice." He glared for a minute, then laughed. "It's more than my little BB-brain wants to think about anyway. I guess they'll get to you sooner or later. It's really weird, isn't it?"

Sam decided not to remind him of last

year's catastrophe when they got her prints. She decided to leave it alone. Ronnie was right about one thing. Whoever they wanted to print would do it or look guilty, one of the two. She passed him his paperwork through the window and then they spent the next fifteen minutes talking about what might have happened to their boss. All the while the policeman listened in . . . Sam felt certain. It didn't matter. One thing both Ronnie and Sam agreed on was they doubted if anyone who worked there killed him.

"We didn't love the guy and we all wished we had a different boss, but none of us would kill him. We didn't want to see the man dead," Ronnie said. "Richardson was a pain, but a pain we'd learned to live with. Besides, none of us are killers. We're just hardworking stiffs who make the government richer by pouring in our tax dollars." He flashed a grin, but not of delight.

"Ain't that the truth?" she said with a chuckle to his remark about the tax dollars. They weren't laughing at the situation. It was a sad state-of-affairs right now. Who would kill Ken? And why?

"They said it happened last night here while you were working. You didn't see or hear anything?" Ronnie dropped his

46

paperwork into his briefcase.

A laugh slipped out of her mouth — not a funny, ha-ha laugh. It was more like hysterical type of laugh you'd hear from someone who was about to go crazy. "Give me a break, Ronnie. You sound like those two policemen who came to my house this morning. But you're right; you'd think if there had been a struggle upstairs, I would have heard something. I mean, I can hear the rats run around upstairs at night. You'd think I would have heard a big man like Ken struggling for his life." She pointed toward the ceiling. "I admit his office is over the drivers' room, not our office, but still, you'd think I would have heard something. But I didn't. And I didn't see anything either. I never sit and watch out the window. At night you can't see much anyway, except headlights when they come into the yard. But again, I'd have to be looking that way to notice. So many of y'all come in and out at night, I don't even pay attention anymore."

"The police came to your house?" Ronnie asked when she finally quit talking.

Sam slapped the heel of her hand against her forehead. "Aye-yi-yi." Throwing her hands out in front of her like two stop signs, she shouted, "Yes! Now, let's change the subject. Please." She dreaded any more talk on the matter. It was too depressing.

Ronnie, being the friend that he was, did as Sam asked. Before he left, he smiled, told a corny Thibodeaux and Boudreaux joke, and then said as he was walking toward the exit, "Keep your chin up, girl. Remember, this won't matter ten years from now." That was Ronnie's favorite line about any problem that arose.

Admittedly, there had been times lately that Sam told herself the same thing. "Yeah, right." The only reason those questions about not hearing or seeing a thing bothered her earlier today was because she was here when it all happened. In her own mind she felt partly responsible for not doing anything to stop Ken from being killed — only she didn't know it was going on at the time. She truly never heard a thing.

Sam knew, no matter how she felt about her boss, she would have done everything in her power to save the man, no matter how poorly he had treated her in the past. She loved him through Christ and that gave her reason to always try to do her best for the man as well as always be there for him.

As the door snapped closed after Ronnie's exit, another thought crossed Sam's mind, bringing a smile to her lips. *Around here everyone says if you don't like the way things are going, hang around a bit and they'll change.* Of course, when the change happened, it was usually for the worse, but she simply chose to ignore that part of the saying. *Think positive* was always her motto to live by anyway.

By the time the minute hand neared the twelve as the hour hand closed in on the six, she felt better and better. Maybe today the police would discover something to help them find the true killer or killers. Too bad Matthew wasn't on the case. He'd solve it in no time.

Twelve hours had slipped by slowly that night, probably because there wasn't much to keep her busy. At least now the night was almost over and she would be off for the next three days.

Pat, her relief dispatcher, walked in to take her place. "You look tired, Sam. Rough night?"

She crinkled her nose as she thought how to answer his question. "Work-wise everything is fine. But I'm still a little down about Matthew. I'm not sure how long it will take to get over my loss. And now, with what's going on around here . . ." As her words faded, she shook her head, not even trying to complete her sentence, but the message was clear.

"I know what you mean. But at least you didn't have the circus around you last night like we had yesterday," Pat grumbled. "If it's like that today, I'm going home sick. It's worse than last year . . . probably because that murder was across the street on the levee. We had our fair share of cops in and out of here then, too." He smiled as he rubbed his dark beard. "I guess you don't need to be reminded of that time either. Sorry."

As Pat sat in the chair Sam had vacated, she patted him on the shoulder. "Cheer up. It probably won't be as bad today. Besides, most of the stuff should be going on upstairs. Hopefully after they get all their evidence, the policemen won't be hanging around all night again."

"Did they give you a hard time last night?" he asked as his gaze moved toward the policeman still out there by the bottom of the stairs.

"No. They stood at their post and walked around a little. Occasionally, they talked to one another at the back door of the drivers' room, but they kept it open. That's how they took their bathroom and lunch breaks, too. When one couldn't stand at their post, the other watched both from the open door."

"That's good."

Squeezing his shoulder, she added, "All you'll have to deal with today are the reporters and TV crews." She laughed as he turned, giving her the evil eye.

"You better hope not. If they show up, I'll give them your home address, telling them you were the one on duty. Go ask Sam for the details." He wiggled his dark brows.

"You wouldn't dare."

He smiled a somewhat sinister grin.

She laughed as she backed away, pointing at him. "I'll tell them you did it, so watch out," she warned.

Both of them laughed until the drivers started gathering at the window wanting to know what was so funny.

"Come on, guys, give us something to laugh about, too," Jerry said. "Our day is just starting, Sam. We're not going home like you are."

"My heart bleeds for you, Jer." She patted over her heart with both hands, like fluttering wings.

"Come on, Sam." Jerry's eyes twinkled and his deep dimples beckoned her. "Besides, I just made a pot of coffee. Come have a cup and talk to us. Me and John want to know the straight and skinny. We know you'll tell us the truth."

She shook her head. "Not this morning, guys. I'm tired, and I'm going home." Turning back to Pat, she said, "On that, I'm out of here. Have a good day." She grabbed her purse and headed for the door.

He hollered bye to Sam as she walked out the front door. She even heard him say, "Drive safe."

Unfortunately she didn't make it to her car. Lieutenant Jones and Sergeant Barnett walked toward the door, blocking the path to her car.

"Morning," she said as she started to go around them. They had another man with them today, carrying what looked like a laptop with a handle.

"Got a minute?" Jones asked.

"Do I have a choice?" Sighing, Sam turned around and walked back inside and into the dispatch office with them.

From the drivers' room she heard one of the drivers holler, "I thought you were leaving?" Sam didn't bother to answer them.

To Pat she said, "I didn't make it. Sorry we're doing this in here, but it shouldn't take but a minute."

"No problem," Pat said, even though it didn't sound like his heart was in on his answer. He then turned his back on the group and continued to do his work.

Lieutenant Jones took charge, turning his dark eyes on Sam. "Simon is going to take more prints today. Those guys you mentioned are coming in this morning. We've taken about half the employees' prints and we'll get more today. We'd like to take yours now. But if you refuse, we'll gladly come over in a couple of hours with a court order and get them. If we need to do this the hard way, we can do that. No problem." The lieutenant's hard gaze spoke volumes.

"What's wrong with the ones you got last year?"

Neither seemed to know about what happened last year or didn't care to acknowledge it, and Sam didn't feel like explaining, so she simply shrugged. "Whatever. Go ahead and take them. I have nothing to hide. I've been in Ken's office before, but my guess is it's been a long time."

"Unless someone wiped them clean, they'll be there. But we're not interested in the prints around the room, only the prints we lifted off the clothes the victim wore."

"Great. Still no problem. Just, can you take my prints first? I've worked all night and need to get home and see my son off to school." *Not counting the fact I didn't get any sleep yesterday after you two came to my house.* That she didn't say aloud. When her eyes flicked to Barnett, she saw his crooked smile, and her natural response was to smile back.

Jones even seemed nicer today, or maybe it was because he was asking other people questions, too. Not just her. The fingerprint technician was the one who took care of Sam.

"Hi. I'm Simon Roth. It won't take me but a minute. Computerized," he said as he lifted his machine slightly.

He laid his case on the empty desk back against the inner wall, opened it, and touched a button. A light came on. After he cleaned the glass, he said, "Lay your hand on top of that piece of glass." It was like a scanner on a copier. A purple beam started at the tip of her middle finger and moved slowly down and past the heel of her hand. He pressed a couple of buttons on his keyboard, wiped the screen clean, and then said, "Other hand, please." The light did the same thing again as her left hand laid on the glass.

It took less than a minute and no mess. Modern technology was wonderful. She guessed he was through because he thanked her for her time. Although it was clean and easy, she didn't like it any better. It made her feel like a criminal. She was glad it was over.

Glancing at the detectives, she was glad when they both nodded as if to say, they too were through with her. That made her day. She needed to hurry home. "Bye, again," she said to Pat as she raced out of the dispatch office.

When she passed the bottom of the stairs, she noticed the doors leading to Ken's office were open, and she peered up. A chill rushed down her spine. Ken would never be climbing those steps again.

Swallowing the knot in her throat, she headed out through the glass door to her car.

Chapter 4

In less than half an hour, Sam was home. The light on her machine was flashing. Yes, she who hated talking into machines — even more than she hated listening to the owner say the same spiel before she could leave a message — had one of her own. At least she didn't play a long clip of music before the caller could leave a message. Sam left her messages short and to the point: "We're not in. Leave a message." She couldn't make it any shorter.

Watching the blinking light, she hoped Marty hadn't heard the phone ring or the message that was left. In her heart, she felt certain it was Greg calling back. Hearing the silence in the house led her to believe both Marty and Margaret were still fast asleep.

Sam and Margaret had prearranged, should Sam ever have to call, that she would let it ring once, hang up, and call right back.

That way Margaret didn't have to answer every call that came into the house . . . not that many people called. Usually the calls were telemarketers. This way those unwanted callers would get the machine. Most hung up without leaving a message. Now *that* was a great thing.

"Hi, Sam. I didn't call you last night 'cause I knew you were at work and couldn't truly talk. I'm already up waiting for your call now, so please call me as soon as you get home."

She didn't have to be told twice. Quickly, she punched in his number.

"Hello." A deep, groggy male voice crossed the line and filled her ear.

"I didn't mean to wake you, Greg. I thought you said you were up."

"Morning. I guess I dozed off while waiting. Sorry."

"It's good to hear your voice." She twisted the cord, wrapped it around her finger, then released it, only to start over again. "Thanks for getting back to me."

"You sound scared. What happened? Not another killing across the highway I hope."

"Not across the highway. This time at the terminal. They found my boss dead in his office. And I think the police believe I did it."

"Sam, you've got to be kidding! What have you gotten yourself into now? Your boss is dead, and they think you did it? Why would they think you killed him?"

"Beats me." Hastily she tried to explain. "The only thing I can figure is because he was killed on my watch. I was there working the night shift, and he was killed in his office." Pulling on the cord, she stretched it out again and wrapped it around her fingers one more time. "Of course, I was downstairs. And I swear I never heard a thing. They talk like I should know something, and I'm covering it up." She blew out a gush of air. "Greg, I honestly don't know if they suspect me or not. It's not like they've accused me. But yesterday when they came to my house and were asking me questions, I got this strange ache in the pit of my stomach, if you know what I mean. And this morning when I was leaving work, they had me stay so they could take my prints. I mean, I don't feel threatened by them, because I know I'm innocent. But the way Lieutenant Jones looked at me, it's like he suspects me even if Sergeant Barnett doesn't. I don't know. I'm not sure. But I get this horrible feeling when they question me."

"You said they took your prints? Did they

Mirandize you first?"

"No. We were all asked to volunteer our prints. They said it would help eliminate prints so they could find some fingerprints that don't belong there — and we were supposed to buy that. Well, actually they told the drivers that. When I said my prints are in his office so you will find them, Jones said they are matching prints on him, his clothing, not prints found in the office. Personally, I don't have anything to hide, so I don't need to feel guilty. But they make me feel so uncomfortable." She trembled all over. "So dirty."

"Well, girl, you get some rest. I'll see what I can find out for you. I'll also find you a good criminal lawyer, just in case."

Iced air swooshed through her, as if she were standing in the doorway of a freezer and it was opened and slammed shut. "So you think they suspect me, too? I was hoping you'd tell me not to worry — that they are only following procedure."

"I don't think they necessarily think you're guilty." His voice sounded reassuring and the pitch came across strong and sincere. "But I believe in being prepared. As you said, you were the only one there when he was killed . . . as far as they know. And I've heard the way you talk about him, so

I'm sure one of your friendly drivers have told them how you two don't get along. Besides, it won't hurt to be prepared."

The grit of what felt like sandpaper slid over her eyeballs as she closed them tightly. Sam was so tired. It had been almost thirty-six hours with maybe a one-hour catnap in between. "Greg, I don't know how to thank you. I know you've been busy, probably working on a job for the governor, but I need your help. I don't know where else to turn. If Matthew —"

"Don't you worry. I'm here for you, Sam. Matthew loved you, and he would kill me if I didn't try to help you. Besides, girl, I think a lot of you and Marty both. You're like family to me . . . almost."

"Thanks, Greg. Sorry I woke you. So you better get some rest, too."

"It's been a long three days, but after a shower, I'll be as good as new. Now you get some rest and I'll come by around two. Let Margaret know I'm coming and ask her to wake you — just in case you're still asleep when I get there. That woman watches over you and Marty like a prison guard." He chuckled.

Greg and Matthew both were glad when Sam had found such a wonderful woman to care for Marty. With the odd hours Sam worked, it wasn't easy, but God had brought her this special woman who was now a dear friend, too. Margaret had moved in with Sam and Marty at their apartment.

Sam couldn't help but think again that, had she and Matthew been married before his death and living at his place, then maybe he'd still be alive. Maybe he would have been more alert when he was attacked. She worried the extra drive from her place to his every night with the hours he worked might have been a distraction for him. Why had they waited a whole year to get married when six months would have been enough? Shaking her head, she remembered. She had wanted to make sure marrying Matthew was the right thing for both Marty and her. She sighed and said aloud, "Thanks again, Greg."

"What are you thinking? I hear it in your voice. Talk to me."

She smiled to herself. Greg almost knew her as well as Matthew knew her. "I was just wishing Matthew was still here."

"You and me both, kiddo."

"I know you're going to watch out for us, but . . ." Tears formed in her eyes, but if she allowed them to fall, she wouldn't be able to turn them off. Sam couldn't cry — not now — not when Marty might find her. She would save her tears for the shower. Her son had been through so much in his short life, she didn't need to add to it.

"That is a fact, so don't you worry, hon. Go to sleep and dream about him. That way he'll be with you. Right now I've got to shower and go see some people."

"Thanks, Greg," she said one more time before hanging up the phone. Yes, she could dream about Matthew, and he would reappear. In her dreams she could still find him. The only problem with that was when she woke up, he would be gone, and she'd have to deal with the heartbreak all over again. Sam wasn't sure she could make it through the next time. Caring for Marty was her stronghold, keeping her mind and heart busy. She thanked God for the time she did have with Matthew, but now she had to concentrate on her son and his needs.

Greg was a good man. He'd help her through this new crisis — if she needed it. Hopefully she was jumping the gun and assuming things that weren't true to fact. Maybe the police didn't think she had anything to do with it.

She sighed. What had happened to the positive attitude she usually had? She needed it now more than ever.

Lately, Sam admitted, she hadn't done too

well staying so positive. *Lord, help me. You are my strength.*

Her purpose in life came running down the hall, all smiles and full of energy. "Morning, Momma. I'm so hungry. Can you make biscuits this morning?"

A smile crossed her lips as she soaked in the image of her baby growing up. *He'll be nine next month. They grow up so quickly.*

CHAPTER 5

Greg didn't like the way that sounded. Were the police investigating this crime or had they already decided Samantha's guilt?

"Don't worry, buddy. I'm not going to leave your woman in the lurch." Greg talked as if Matthew sat in the same room with him, but Greg knew better.

To himself he said, "First things first." Greg flipped open his cell. Scanning the names in his contact list, he found who he was looking for, an old friend still on the force. Lieutenant James Draper chose to spend the last of his days before retirement working a desk job. After the injury to his leg a year ago, he could have taken an early retirement with a reduced pension. Instead, James decided to ride his time out behind a desk. It wasn't the real grunt work of police procedure, but it kept him on the force full-time so he could retire in another three years at his full pension. Now Greg hoped

James, Jimmy to his friends, hadn't changed his mind. For all Greg knew, the new position behind a desk all day bored him to no end. His old buddy might not be willing to share the info Greg really needed, but he had to try.

Tapping his friend's name on his phone, the man's cell number appeared on the screen, and Greg tapped it, too. Instantly the phone keyed in the number and a ringing tone sounded.

"Lieutenant Draper. May I help you?"

"Hey, Jimmy, old boy. It's me, Greg. I hope you can help me." Greg hoped more so that he would *want* to help him. Greg knew Jimmy could get his hands on most of the information in the case, but it was against policy to talk to anyone outside the force about the facts of an ongoing investigation. "Can you spare me a few minutes? I need to come see you right away."

"You sound serious, Greg. Is the governor giving you a hard time? Are you thinking of coming back to the force?" Adding a little merriment to his voice, Jimmy said, "I'll tell you what. Bring some doughnuts and we can talk."

"You're on. Do you still like the powdery ones filled with strawberry goo?"

"I may be a gimp, but I still have my taste buds. Bring 'em on."

By the time Greg picked up the doughnuts and drove to the precinct almost forty-five minutes had passed. The doughnuts were hot and fresh since that had been his last stop before reaching the precinct. That should score him a few extra points. Greg nodded at some of the officers as he passed and made his way toward Jimmy's desk. That was the thing most policemen didn't like about a desk job. Everyone was in a large room with several desks, and you had very little privacy, if any. But with the noise level of the computers, copiers, and faxes all humming, as well as the low chatter from various desks, no one paid much attention to all the conversations going on at the same time. So, in a way, they had privacy.

As Greg reached Jimmy's desk and was about to drop the box in front of him, the tall thin man rose and stuck out his right hand, welcoming the intrusion. "I don't care what you need. I'm just glad to have the break in the monotony of taking complaints of noisy neighbors or reports of cats stuck in trees. Good to see you, Greg." Jimmy shook Greg's hand almost off of him.

"Hey, old man. Glad to see you, too. You're looking good. No stress lines across the face. The desk job might be boring but at least it lets you go home at night not worrying about catching some perp before he kills again. Right?"

"You got that right. My wife is grateful for that."

Pulling his hand back, Greg grabbed the chair next to the desk and dragged it a little closer before sitting down. "I've got a big favor to ask of you."

Plopping his skinny self back in his chair, Jimmy rolled closer to his desk again and opened the box of doughnuts. Smacking his lips, he said, "Whatever I can do for you, buddy." He glanced up at Greg and then back at the doughnuts. "You name it." His fingers plucked a confection-covered delectable out of the box and raised it to his lips. "Mmm," he moaned in delight before taking a big bite.

Greg set his elbow on the corner of the desk and leaned toward Jimmy. "You remember Matthew's fiancée, Samantha Cain?"

"Uh huh," he mumbled as he chewed.

"Well, her boss was killed, and it sounds to her like the police are suspecting her."

Jimmy swallowed his mouthful of doughnut and gulped a little coffee behind it. "Really, man! Isn't that how Matthew

67

met her to begin with? Wasn't she in some kind of trouble after a killing happened over by her workplace?"

"Close enough." Greg didn't want to go into details and remind him she was the widow of a fellow officer who took his own life and Matthew was that policeman's partner at the time. Jimmy didn't need to be reminded. So many of the men in blue weren't very friendly toward her in the beginning, according to what Matthew had told Greg.

"Problem is, she didn't do it, even though it's a well-known fact she didn't get along with her boss," Greg said. "She was at the place where his body was found. So to me, it sounds like the police may have motive and opportunity wrapped up with a ribbon on top. Too simple. Too easy. I don't know about means. Sam isn't even sure how the man died, just that they found him dead in his office the morning after she worked the night shift. She never saw anyone come or go. She had no idea he was upstairs dead when she left to go home after a night on the job. Unfortunately this makes her a prime suspect."

Jimmy finished off the first doughnut and was going for the second one when he said, "It sounds like she might be in a little trouble." His gaze drifted from the doughnut box to Greg. "Again."

"Exactly. That's what I'm hoping you can check out for me. See how much. Take a look, ask around, and see if they are set on her, or if they are still investigating. It seems to me all the evidence against her is circumstantial." He shrugged. "Actually sounds like someone planned it that way."

Swallowing the last of his second doughnut, Jimmy took time for another gulp of coffee. With a thoughtful look he said, "I'll see what I can find out, but I'm not promising anything. Understand?"

Rising, Greg stuck out his hand and they shook. "I appreciate whatever you can do. Sam has been through so much. Remember, Matthew was killed a week before their wedding, and the woman is still grieving deeply. Not to mention her son, Marty. He loved Matthew like a dad. I don't think he needs to have his mother arrested for something she didn't do."

Jimmy rose and clapped Greg on the back of his right shoulder. "I gotcha. I'll get back to you right away." With a limp, Jimmy started walking through the room around the desks with Greg.

"Thanks again, Jimmy. You have my cell. Call me any time, day or night." They shook hands one more time before parting ways.

Back in his car, Greg started the engine, fastened his seat belt, and pulled his cell out of his top pocket. Slipping it into the holder, he pressed the button to speed-dial Sam's home number, and then clicked on SPEAKER.

"Cain residence. May I help you?"

"Well, good morning, Margaret. Don't you sound all peaches and cream this morning?"

"Oh, Mr. Greg. Hush yourself." She giggled.

"I can see you blushing without being there, Margaret. And quit calling me Mr. Greg. It's plain old Greg. Do you hear me?" Greg gritted his teeth when he realized he was flirting with Margaret while Sam was waiting for some news — preferably good. "Is Sam awake?" He decided to keep his mind on business.

"She's napping but told me to wake her when you called. Have you found out something that will help her? Are you coming over?" Margaret's interest was made clear on the phone. She cared so much for Samantha and Marty, it was upsetting her to see them go through more tragedy. Greg knew without a doubt, Margaret had a huge heart.

"I'm on my way. I don't have much to tell her yet, but I thought I'd come over and we could discuss the situation more, face-to-face." He slid the gears into reverse and backed out of the parking space. "I'll be there in about ten minutes or so . . . if that's okay."

"I'll put on a fresh pot of coffee, wake her up, and start cooking some breakfast for both of you. When she gets up, she'll stay up. Ms. Sam's off for the next three days. She rarely sleeps more than four hours anyway when she's coming up on the long weekend. And under the circumstances, the hour and a half sleep she's had will probably be all the sleep she'll need today. That way, tonight, she'll be back on track with Marty's schedule."

"Margaret, you know they say the way to a man's heart is through his stomach, and woman, you are on the fast track to mine." He did it again. What had gotten into him? Every time he got near that woman he acted like a schoolboy. Greg thought his flirting days were over.

"Oh, Mr. Gr— I mean, plain old Greg." She chuckled. "You quit that. Come on over. Ms. Sam will be up when you get here."

After a quick laugh, Greg pushed the gas

pedal a little harder. "I'm on my way, woman."

CHAPTER 6

Sam heard a light tapping on her bedroom door. As it opened slightly, she heard, "Sorry to wake you so soon, but Mr. ah . . . Greg is on his way. He'll be here shortly. I brought you a cup of coffee to help you wake up." Margaret moved toward the bed and set the cup on the nightstand.

As Sam opened her eyes slowly, Margaret's words started to sink into her sleepy brain. Her eyes popped open. Suddenly she felt wide-awake and sat up in bed. "Did he give you any idea of what he found?" Hope fluttered in her heart as anticipation climbed. Glancing at the numbers glowing on her digital clock, she realized not even two hours had passed since she'd talked to him that morning. "Wow. That was quick. I hope it's good news."

"Sorry. He hasn't found anything out yet, but he wanted to talk face-to-face and get some details. I'm sure he's been checking into things already this morning. As much as possible, anyway."

Tossing back the covers, Sam eased over and sat on the edge of her bed as she took the cup from the nightstand. "You're right. I'm sure he's doing all he can. And I'm grateful." Sipping cautiously on the hot brew, she looked up. "Thanks."

"I'm making breakfast for you and Mr. Greg . . . uh, Greg, so hurry and get up. Now let me get back to cooking." Margaret scurried from the bedroom.

Sam rose from her bed sipping more of her coffee. Oh, how she wished Matthew was still around to hold her and assure her everything would be all right, but he wasn't. She shook her head, trying to remove those thoughts. The sooner she accepted that she was on her own, the sooner she could move on with her life. Instantly her heart assured her, *You're not on your own. The Lord will never leave nor forsake you. And look at the great friends you have. And most of all, remember Marty needs you to be strong and there for him. You will never be alone.*

"I just miss you, Matthew. You were my rock," she whispered upward for a moment. *And now,* her mind shouted at her, *get busy. Get dressed before Greg gets here.*

Padding to the bathroom connected to her

bedroom, she yawned and put her cup on the counter. Sam leaned over and splashed the cold running water on her face. She needed all the help she could get to wake up quickly. With the little sleep she'd had in the last two days, it would probably take a little miracle. She'd take that, too, a miracle. A grin touched her lips as the reflection in the mirror showed her face dripping in water. Snatching the hand towel off the rack, she dabbed her face dry. "That helped."

After two more gulps of coffee, she stripped and showered. Wrapping a towel around her, soaking up any drops she might have missed when toweling dry, she stepped back into her bedroom and dressed. Once her teeth were brushed and her hair was combed, she felt ready to face the world . . . well at least face the day.

"Something smells good," she said as she entered the kitchen with her empty coffee cup. Margaret had set the table for two. When the doorbell rang, Sam said, "If you don't mind letting Greg in, I'll pour myself another cup."

"Sure," Margaret said as she rushed through the swinging kitchen door.

Sam glanced at the door, still swinging, with curiosity. Margaret's face had flushed when the doorbell chimed and then she raced to answer it. Was something stirring between Margaret and Greg? Sam smiled, deciding to take better note of the two in the future.

To Sam's ears, the conversation in the living room seemed to be of a jovial nature. Even more reason to believe that Margaret's blush had a reason for being there. After the last twenty-four hours, Sam was glad to hear someone laughing. In that instant, she realized she need not concern herself as much as she had with the situation surrounding her life. Her existence was in God's hands, and He wouldn't give her any more than she could handle. That was a promise from Him. Sometimes Sam believed God gave her a little too much credit, but she knew the fire she walked through with God's help only refined and strengthened her. The Word told her so. Besides, she'd lived through enough to know God was in control. Not her. His way was higher than hers.

The kitchen door swung open and stayed. Greg held it that way, allowing Margaret entrance. Both were smiling brightly. Greg sniffed the air. "My stomach hears you, dear, loud and clear. What did you make for breakfast?"

"Nothing special. I promise. I whipped up a couple of egg, cheese, and onion omelets, then sliced some of that ham I baked the other night. I warmed it up in a skillet."

"You don't have to tempt me anymore. I'm ready to eat." He rubbed his stomach. "I'm famished."

"I'm guessing that's a good thing, Greg. It looks like Margaret's got it all ready for us. You better be hungry. Look at all the food."

Margaret scurried over to the oven and lifted a pan. Quickly, she slid her spatula under one omelet and laid it on a plate. As she was doing the same thing with the other omelet, she said, "You two sit down and eat before it gets cold." A plate of hot, lightly browned ham sat in the middle of the table and beside it was a stack of buttered toast. "Do you want milk with your breakfast or just coffee?" The question, although she didn't call them by name, was addressed to both.

"Coffee's enough for me," said Sam.

"If it's not too much trouble, I'll take a glass of milk with my breakfast and then I'll drink a cup of the coffee for dessert." Greg slipped into the chair with his back to the outside door and his face toward the living room. "You spoil me, Margaret."

A rosy glow spread across her cheeks

again, and her eyes twinkled.

There goes the blushing again, and look at Greg. He lit up while talking with Margaret. Maybe there is something going on. Wouldn't that be nice?

Sam blessed the food, then said, "You are going to join us, aren't you, Margaret? Greg is going to give us an update on what he's found out."

"Please do, Margaret," Greg said as he pointed to a chair to his right, across from Sam. "But I hate to say, I really don't have anything yet. Sam, I want you to give me details on what exactly went down at your place of work for the last couple of days." Stuffing a bite of the egg creation into his mouth, he emitted a low murmur of pure pleasure as he started chewing and closed his eyes. After several seconds ticked by, he swallowed slowly, appearing to savor every last flavor of the morsel. Opening his eyes, he said, "Margaret, this omelet is very tasty. Thanks so much for including me in the breakfast feast."

"Thank you," Margaret whispered.

"Greg is so right. Margaret, this is delicious," Sam said as she cut another bite off her slice of the ham. "And Greg, don't worry. I knew you didn't have anything. Margaret told me when she woke me up a little while ago. I'm still a little groggy, but I'll catch up. I think it's called sleep deprivation." Sam slipped another bite of the ham into her mouth and enjoyed the flavor of honey and ham.

Margaret fixed herself a cup of coffee and joined the two at the table.

As Sam ate, between bites she rehashed the last two nights of trauma at her job. She finished her breakfast long before she had replayed all the details. "I don't understand how they could think I would kill my boss. I wouldn't kill anyone, unless maybe Marty's life depended on it. My dad told me a long time ago, you never know what you'll do until you're put in a situation where you have to react fast, so never say never." Sliding her chair back, she rose and stepped over to the coffee pot to pour herself another cup. "Are you ready for your dessert, Greg?" She chuckled. "Margaret, may I fix you another cup, too?"

"Don't mind if I do, please," said Greg as he handed his empty cup over to Sam.

"I've had enough coffee for now, thanks anyway," Margaret said.

As Sam placed a cup of the brew on the table near Greg, he said, "I wish I had some answers for you. I'm not even sure why they are looking so closely at you. I understand you were the only one there most of the night, but most people wouldn't believe you did it given his size alone. So why do they? Why do you think they are focusing on you?"

Sam shrugged. "Beats me."

"One good thing I can say, I did get to talk to my old buddy, Jimmy, who is still on the force. He promised to see what he could do to get some information for me — share what he can without crossing the line. An ongoing investigation is usually kept close to the vest."

Margaret rose and picked up the empty plates from the table. As she carried them to the counter, she said, "I've seen her boss before. He is one big man. Unless Sam shot him or drugged him, I don't see her getting the upper hand on the man. How was he killed, anyway? Did your friend know? Besides, don't the police have to have motive, means, and opportunity to arrest someone? This whole thing makes no sense to me." Margaret's curls bounced as she shook her head.

"When I left Jimmy, he was going to check into any and everything he could find out about the case. Then he said he'd let me know what he could. We'll see what happens."

Sam helped clear the table as Margaret started rinsing the dishes and loading them into the dishwasher. While moving the glass and silverware from table to counter, Sam's gaze slid over Greg. "I hope your friend can help, but I realized a short time ago I shouldn't be worrying. God is in control. I'm glad He has given me two wonderful people who care so much about me to help me step in the right direction through this whole mess —"

Greg's phone chimed six quick successive dings, repeating over and over, cutting Sam's words short. He reached in his pocket and pulled out his phone. The dings stopped as he said, "Singleton here."

Sam and Margaret both turned and waited. Sam pinched the edge of the table with her fingers as her eyes stayed glued on Greg's face, while Margaret seemed to be holding her breath. Seconds turned into long minutes, more than Sam wanted to wait. As soon as Greg pressed the button to end the call, she said, "What'd he say? What'd he find out?"

Greg rose. "I have to go back down to the station, but he said it didn't look good. He suggested you get yourself a good lawyer."

Sam's heart stopped beating as Margaret gasped. When Sam found her breath, she whispered, "Get myself a lawyer? But I didn't do anything." She snatched hold of Margaret's fingertips and held on tight.

Catching Sam's upper arms in a tight hold, Greg said, "Hang in there, girl. It'll be okay."

The phrase *innocent until proven guilty* flashed through her mind. But then she remembered Christ was innocent, and they still hung Him on a cross. Then she thought how foolish to even compare her life to Christ's. He had a great purpose. God had a plan. Without Jesus suffering on the cross, we would not be saved for eternity. *So what purpose is there for them to find me guilty when I'm not?*

Suddenly a peace washed over her as she remembered, *God is in control.* She hadn't been found guilty. The police were checking out her story. Whatever lay ahead, she would get through it with the Lord on her side.

Taking in a deep breath, she stood straight. "Thanks," she whispered to Greg and then walked him to the front door as Margaret followed along with them.

CHAPTER 7

Mark Barnett looked over his notes of all the interviews they'd conducted in the last thirty-six hours and studied the pictures of the crime scene.

The interviews of the workers all kept to basically the same story. Each employee started out as a strong defender of their boss's reputation, but in the end admitted to the fact that not too many people cared for the way he handled the terminal. Richardson wasn't a very well liked man. Now when it came to what they had to say about Samantha Cain, it was nothing but glowing words for a wonderful coworker.

The drivers loved the way she looked out for them. Her fellow dispatchers liked the way she did her job and that she was always willing to help them when they felt overwhelmed with work. Since she'd been working the night shift, they missed her personality . . . and help . . . on the days.

Some immediately shared how the boss treated her so poorly. Ken apparently didn't like having a woman as a dispatcher. Some employees they had to pry it out of, but in the end, the story was still the same. None understood how Sam put up with Ken's treatment of her. She didn't deserve it, but Ken Richardson didn't seem to care. In fact, most said he hoped she would quit.

Studying the pictures one at a time, he felt he was missing something. He felt a churning in the back of his mind . . . as if he'd noticed something, but his rational thoughts hadn't connected it yet. What was it? Something missing? Or something there that shouldn't be? He sighed, wishing he knew.

Sitting back in his chair, he glanced across his desk at his partner. He'd love to share his thoughts, knock some ideas around, but, to Ben Jones, the case was already solved. He wanted to hang Samantha Cain out to dry.

Mark sat up slightly and leaned forward a bit, eyeing his partner. Something was going on over there in Ben's mind. What, he didn't know. The lieutenant's mind was fixed on something. "Share partner," Mark said. "What are you looking at so intently?" *Let's try to act like partners.* Jones appeared

84

to be staring through his computer screen. This got Mark's full attention.

"We just got the results on all trace evidence, including all the prints we had taken. Guess who's on top?" Jones pressed a button on his screen, and the printer hummed as it kicked on automatically.

Jones had the biggest smile, so Mark didn't have to guess who was on top. The man never smiled. He shook his head as he said, "It must be Ms. Cain's. You wouldn't look so happy otherwise. What do you have against her? You're like," he lifted both hands in question, "I don't know, man. You're convicting her before you get all the evidence. I don't get you, Ben. In fact, I've never seen you act like this on a case before. What gives?"

Jones pulled the report off the printer and dropped a copy on his partner's desk. "Check it out. See where her prints were found."

Mark picked up the paper and scanned the names of the prints found in the office and where they were found. "Gimme a break." He tossed the paper back down on his desk as if it was of no consequence. "We knew we'd find her prints on the letter opener. It belonged to the dispatchers. Remember? I'm sure her prints weren't the only ones found."

The smile broadened as he cocked his head. "Think again."

"That's too easy." Jumping to his feet, Mark snatched his blazer off the back of his chair, hooking it with his finger. "Let's go do some real detective work. Like finding out more about our victim and who would want him dead. Then we can talk to other possible suspects. And then let's wait until all the facts and evidence are in before making an arrest. Let's wait on the results on the hair sample for one thing. Besides, we really do need to find out a little more about this man and his life. Listening to all the coworkers, it's not like he was an innocent man. It sounded like he was one of those men who did some jobs under the table. I'm sure we'll find more people who didn't like him, besides just the people who worked with him."

"Yeah. But will we find their prints on the letter opener, the weapon used to stab him in the heart? The weapon we found tossed out back in the big garbage bin?" Another smile, this time more of a smirk. "Let's go chase some other possible suspects. I don't want to be accused of focusing only on her when we do finally get to go and arrest the woman." A bellow of laughter escaped as he pulled the car keys from his pocket. "I'm ready."

If they hadn't been partners for the past five years, Mark wouldn't have known what a truly good detective Jones could be. Right now Mark wanted to smack him upside the head. Maybe that would knock some sense into him.

What does he have against Ms. Cain? Matthew, a fellow detective, had thought the world of her — had been ready to marry her — yet Jones thought she was a killer. Mark would have to work harder at finding other viable suspects before Jones hung her out to dry.

As they were about to leave, his partner's office phone rang. Stepping back over to his desk he snatched up the receiver. "Jones here." His eyes widened as he listened to whoever was talking to him. His gaze seemed to brighten with every word.

Mark's heart tightened. Jones' expression could only mean bad news for Samantha Cain. Mark stood waiting for Jones to hang up the phone so he could crow a little more. At least that was the impression Mark received from the look on Jones' face.

"Thanks." Jones slammed down the receiver. "Let's go. The ME has something else for us." He jabbed his fist up into the air. "Yes. Maybe this will be the clincher I was hoping for." Then he drew his fist in and downward in one smooth motion.

All Mark could do was follow the man downstairs, dreading what the medical examiner was about to share with them.

CHAPTER 8

Three hours passed before Greg returned, and he wasted no time joining Sam and Margaret at the kitchen table. He took a seat and laid a file on the tabletop. Opening it, he revealed some printed papers along with photos. Sam couldn't help but try to tilt her head slightly to see the photos.

Shocked, she pointed to the one on top. "That's mine." The police had a picture of her necklace . . . her misplaced necklace. "Matthew gave that to me. Who's holding it, and what's it doing in a folder you brought back from the police station?"

She didn't understand. How could someone have her necklace? Even more, why was it in that picture? Since Matthew had given it to her, she'd worn it all the time, only taking it off at home at night when she went to bed. Every morning she had put it back on until a few months ago. Sam couldn't even say how long it had been. With the loss of Matthew, her mind was on other matters these past few months, but she knew it would turn up one day safe and sound in her own home. Truth be told, she figured it had dropped behind her dresser. One day she planned to pull that heavy thing out from the wall and look behind it. That, like other things, had been put on her list of things to do when she moved on in her life. Since his death, she had concentrated on caring for her son and working. That was about it, and that was how she got through one day at a time.

"That's the bad news, hon. Ken Richardson was found clutching it tightly. The ME had to pry his fingers loose. That was what the report said." Flipping through the papers, Greg pulled the report out and laid it in front of her. "So it seems, according to the response from the detectives, he snatched it off the killer's neck. Look at the clasp. It's broken." He picked up the pictures and laid them out. "These are copies of the crime scene photos. Look at this close-up of the chain — snapped in two. Obviously they don't know it's yours yet, but they are asking questions. As soon as Jimmy heard the buzz, he thought I'd want to know, so he added it to the file he was making for me. I thought I recognized it when he showed me that picture. I wasn't sure if it was yours or not. I never said a word to Jimmy. Just thanked him for his help."

"Oh no!" she cried out. The tight squeeze on her heart crept up to her throat, choking off her oxygen supply. "How did he get my necklace? It disappeared a few months ago." She laid her hand on her chest and dragged in a deep breath of air, forcing her lungs to expand and then, just as quickly, released it. "I figured I misplaced it one night before going to bed or it fell behind furniture, or something. I knew one day it would show up again. I wasn't worried. It's not like I ever took the necklace off anywhere except here at the house . . . well, and at our apartment before we moved here. I presumed one day it would show up down in the couch or behind a dresser or somewhere. But here in our home, not there."

Margaret reached over and patted Sam's hand. "It will be okay, Ms. Sam. Greg will help you figure this out." Her eyes shot a glance toward Greg, and then she lowered her lashes.

Sam fastened her gaze once more on the photos, wrestling with worry, fear, and confusion. She wasn't sure which emotion described her feelings best as she soaked in each picture, each shot. Seeing Ken lying on the floor, looking at peace, his hands balled up into fists at his side twisted her stomach. He was dead. That big man, who stopped others dead in their tracks with a look or a word, was lying there lifeless. So not like Ken Richardson. The close up of his hand holding the necklace, apparently taken later by the ME, and then various shots of the necklace, close-ups of the body, close-ups of the necklace, followed with pictures of the rest of his office in its entirety left her wordless. Finally with raised eyes she said, "What do we do, Greg? What do I do?"

"Margaret's right. I'll help you. We both will help you, and you'll get through this, too. First thing we're going to do is find you the best defense attorney there is — not that you'll need him or her. Somehow the police will find the true killer and if they don't, we will! You're not taking the fall for this, kiddo. Trust me."

Sam couldn't believe this was happening again. Maybe it wasn't the same thing. It wasn't like a killer stalked her again like last year, but now — now she might be snatched away from her son. For murder, no less. That could mean life in prison. Sam knew her parents would step in and raise Marty if it came to that, but that wasn't the point. She wanted to raise her son, watch him grow up, be with him his entire life. Besides, Marty had already lost his father and his soon-to-be stepfather. He shouldn't have to lose his mother, too.

"Thank you, Greg and Margaret. You don't know how much you mean to me. I appreciate your help so much. Let's get started. The sooner we clear me, the sooner we can get on with our lives." She started to rise, but Greg laid his hand on top of hers, stopping her actions.

"Let me make a few calls." Greg padded over to the counter where the house phone sat. He pulled out the phonebook that rested under the handset and carried it to the table. Flipping through the white pages, he found who he was looking for and started punching the numbers into his cell phone. "This should only take a minute."

Margaret stood and then in a soft voice said, "While Greg takes care of finding you the perfect person to protect you, I'm going to pick up the house. You know I'm here for you, and if you have to go anywhere with Mr. ah, with Greg, don't you worry about Marty. I'm here, and that's where I'm staying." She wrapped her arms around Sam's neck, gave her a quick squeeze, and then left the room.

Sam fixed herself and Greg another cup of coffee. By the time she finished and sat back down, Greg was finishing his call. His eyes locked with hers and he said, "We've got an appointment." He glanced at his watch. "We need to be there in about one hour. Finish this cup, then go get ready. My buddy gave me a great attorney's name earlier. She used to work for the DA so she should be sharp and know all the angles. She should be able to tell me what we can do to help the police find the real killer instead of settling on you as the scapegoat. That's all you are, you know. An easy, *let's close this case and put it behind us,* answer for the cops. We're not going to allow that to happen, Samantha. Don't you worry! Matthew wouldn't let it happen, and neither will I. I'll make sure we find the true killer." Greg slapped the table, pitched her a crooked grin, and then picked up his cup and took a swig of coffee. Winking, he said, "Trust me, kiddo."

"I do." Sam's shoulders relaxed a little as she took another swallow of her coffee. "I do," she repeated and then set her cup back down on the table.

An hour later, Sam and Greg sat in the waiting room of Claire Marie Babineaux, Attorney at Law. They didn't wait long before the receptionist said, "Ms. Babineaux will see you now." She rose and stepped around her desk and then led them to her boss's door. Opening it, the woman stepped back, giving Greg and Samantha room to walk in, and then the receptionist closed the door behind them.

The lawyer was already moving toward the door to greet them. Extending her hand, she said, "How do you do? Please, have a seat." She motioned them toward the two chairs facing her desk.

As they sat down, Greg said, "You came highly recommended by a friend of mine from down at the courthouse. This is Samantha Cain, the lady I spoke of on the phone."

"Tell me again what you've been charged with," Claire said, directing her question toward Samantha.

"Oh!" Sam's hands flew up as if in surrender. Her voice in a higher pitch than normal squeaked as she said, "I haven't been charged yet. And hopefully I won't." Her heart raced at the thought of being arrested.

"We're trying to be a little proactive here," Greg explained as he clamped a hand down on Sam's shoulder and patted her gently. "It's okay," he whispered. "I used to work for the police department and a friend of mine on the force gave me a little heads-up when I started asking questions. Sam, tell Ms. Babineaux what happened."

Sam gathered her thoughts. "Okay. Two homicide detectives came to my house yesterday morning after I had worked the night shift. I'm a dispatcher at a trucking company. The detectives asked all kinds of questions and then finally let me know that my boss, Ken Richardson, was found dead in his office that morning. I worked the night shift and was basically the only one there most of the night."

"So this is a case of being in the wrong place at the wrong time?" Claire asked. "Is that what you're telling me? Police usually have a pretty strong case before the DA tells them to make an arrest. Why — besides the fact you were there the night he apparently was killed — did they pick you?"

Greg handed Claire the file folder. "Inside you'll find pictures of the crime scene, as well as some of the notes made by the first officer on the scene. I don't have anything the detectives have said, other than the note made after the ME's picture of the necklace found in his hand, but that was enough to make me feel we needed to take action. Samantha is innocent."

The lawyer's eyes were noncommittal as she glanced at Samantha before looking down at the file in her hands.

Sam watched the attorney scan the statements made by the police officer at the scene. She wanted to speak out in her own defense but knew now was not the time. Next the woman's eyes scrutinized each picture one at a time. "I see they mention you being there all night long and that you heard no one upstairs where the body was found. Is this true?"

"Yes, but I didn't do it." Sam wanted to shout but forced herself to remain calm. "Some drivers came in and went out, passing through, you might say, during the night — but I never heard anything from upstairs. Not that I can recall, anyway. Besides, upstairs is always locked at night. The only part anyone can get into is the upstairs storage section out back. Some of the major parts for our trucks are stored there. Other than that, the shop foreman and the boss both have offices upstairs with separate entrances. There is a door, however, that separates the two offices. The boss's office you enter at the top of the stairs on the side of the drivers' room and the shop foreman's office you enter from the back stairs in the shop. For all three doors there is a key. Three different keys. Keys only held by Ken, the boss, and Otto, the shop foreman."

"And you say you didn't hear anything upstairs?"

"No, I didn't. I reminded the homicide detectives that Ken's office was over the drivers' room, not the dispatcher's. Besides, I don't have a key to any of those doors I mentioned."

"And you told them that? So why are they still focusing on you?"

Sam looked at Greg, not sure what to say next. She had no true idea why they would focus on her. She was there all night. Yes, it was true they didn't get along. But she would never kill him. Besides the fact he was so big, how would she ever get the upper hand on that man even if she wanted to?

He nodded. "Tell her everything. You know — how he treated you different."

Whoosh. A long slow gush of air released. "Okay. First, because I was the one there — opportunity. Second, because the boss and I didn't get along too well over the past couple of years. Motive, I guess? Third, because his wife said he came to the office because I called him . . . but I didn't. More opportunity. Lastly, and they don't even know this but we do, that necklace he's holding in his hand is mine. When they find that out, they really will be circling the wagons for me." Her hands made two fists. "I know I sound guilty — with all that, I mean. How can they not help but think I'm guilty? Wrapped up with a pink bow and ready for slaughter." Sam wanted to cry. Pressing her fingers against her lips, she tried to hold back the sobs that threatened to escape. After she said all of this to the attorney, how could the woman not think she was the guilty party, too? Discouragement hung like a cloud over her head.

"And the preliminary report stated he died from a stab wound. They discovered a bloody letter opener out back in the shop in the big garbage can. The weapon had a partial print. It matched Sam's fingerprints," Greg added.

"Means." Sam's voice was low, and her shoulders drooped. They had enough to put her away for life. She didn't want to go to jail. She couldn't; she had to be there for her son. Locking her tear-filled eyes on the lawyer, she said, "But that's the dispatcher's letter opener . . . all the dispatchers. Not just mine. We keep it in the dispatch office in the pencil holder. All the other dispatchers who use it should have their prints on it as well," Sam added in her defense. "I noticed last week the opener was missing."

"Did you tell anyone? Or did anyone else notice it and tell you?" asked Claire.

"I left a note for the secretary, asking her to get us another one. I told her someone must have walked off with it. That happens all the time with our pens and paperclips, so she was used to ordering things again for us. We've even had staplers walk off over the years." Sam wrung her hands in her lap.

"One thing stood out to me when I glanced over the police officer's notes. When he went to notify the wife of her husband's death, on his follow-up questions he wrote that the wife stated you called him out to work," Claire said. "And you said a moment ago that wasn't true. Did you tell the detectives you never called him that night?"

"Yes, I did. I told them emphatically that I did not call the boss! I try to never call him at night. Only in case of a bad accident would I disturb him at home."

"So why is his wife lying?"

Shaking her head, Sam said, "She's not. Not Dorothy. She wouldn't do that. She and I have always gotten along well. Maybe Ken told her I called, using me as an excuse to slip out at night. I don't know what that man does away from work. There is no telling what he does or who he sees." Frowning, she added, "Not that I've ever thought he was unfaithful to his wife before. Don't get me wrong. I'm not trying to give the man a bad reputation or ruin his memory. I'm just trying to give you a reason why she might think I called."

Silence filled the room as Claire Babineaux glanced over the paperwork one more time and then the pictures one at a time. Sam watched in silence but finally turned her eyes on Greg, hoping to get an inkling of an idea of what he thought the lawyer might be thinking. She needed something good to cling to before she went home to Marty. She couldn't have him go through another major ordeal in his life.

Please, Lord, give this woman wisdom to clear my name of this charge, should they bring it against me. After lifting a prayer to the Lord, she glanced at Greg again.

He was studying the lawyer but then, seeming to sense Sam's eyes on him, turned in her direction. He gave her a half smile and a reassuring nod.

There was the hope. She waited longer for the lawyer to break the silence.

Finally Claire said, "I think I can help you. And I agree in jumping on this right away.

My thoughts are that the DA isn't far from making an arrest. All this evidence the officer speaks of seems pretty good. But I'm sure they will get with you on some of these things to see if you can explain any of them. They'll want to be sure. Some of it is circumstantial, but when they discover that necklace is yours, they'll really feel good about their evidence. So remember, the next time they want to talk to you, don't do it without me. Here's my card. Put me on your speed dial." She rose as if she was saying good-bye at the same time.

Sam stood as she took the card. Greg rose as he said, "Remember, Ms. Babineaux, I was a policeman for many years. I want to help do any detective work I can . . . help point the police in the right direction. Sam is not the killer, so the best defense should be the police finding the true killer, even if they need me to point them in the right direction."

Claire smiled. "I do have an investigator, you know. I've been doing this job for some time. First as an Assistant DA and then I stepped out on my own. But I felt led to help the innocent. Working for the DA for ten years like I did, I believe, helps me be a better defense attorney. Not bragging, just stating a fact." She pulled another card out of her business card holder and held it out in Greg's direction.

"That's why we came to you. We need the best." Greg took the card and then shook her hand.

Sam swallowed hard as Ms. Babineaux extended her right hand in Samantha's direction. Shaking it, she said thank you to the lawyer, but to the Lord she said, *Here we go again. I'm so sorry, but lead me in every step of the way. Help me prove my innocence. Lead Greg and my lawyer in all the right steps also.*

Could things get worse? She prayed they wouldn't.

Chapter 9

Sam climbed in Greg's car. Her back erect, rigid while she waited for him.

He clambered in, put the key in the ignition, and turned it. The motor purred to life.

"Now what?" she asked. "Do we go home and wait on the lawyer to tell us our next move?" The harder she thought about the next move, the less she could think straight. Was there hope for her? Could she get out of this mess? She was innocent, but how could she prove it?

Slipping the gears into reverse, Greg said, "No. We need to try and gather a little information about Ken Richardson. You only know Ken the boss. We need to find out what and whom he was involved with away from the job, as well as things that might have gone on through the job that you wouldn't know anything about. We'll go back to your place and you can make a list of the friends' names you do know. Hopefully, through them, we can get some leads to start tracking."

Shaking her head, she said, "I can think of some of his friends he brought around the office or who called, but they were his friends. They didn't want to kill him."

Darting his eyes in her direction, Greg said, "Kiddo, I know you think the man was well liked by everyone who didn't work for him, but obviously someone didn't like him. They didn't like him enough to kill him. That's a pretty strong dislike."

"You're right." She concentrated. "There are two local friends and an old buddy who calls him pretty regularly from Alabama. Well, they did when I worked the day shift."

"That's a start. We'll see what we can get from them."

"But Greg, those are his friends. Do you really think they'll give up information to us that easily? Especially if they know I'm a suspect. Wouldn't they try to cover up things they knew about their buddy? I mean, anything negative about him. You know, to protect his memory." Sam clasped her hands together to keep from wringing them. Oh, how she wished this wasn't happening, even though she believed in her heart all would end well. Surely God would not let her be found guilty of something she didn't do. She was innocent. Ken's friends probably wouldn't tell Sam anything, but she needed to help find the information. Somehow, someway. Sam didn't want to wait around while the police and Greg did all the work. She wanted — needed — to do her part.

"First the list, and then we see how they respond to me. I think it's best you're not with me when I question his best friends. They may already realize you are a person of interest to the police, so they probably wouldn't want to help you. I don't have to let them know I'm working on your behalf." He flashed her a bright smile.

"But I can't sit around doing nothing."

Greg spared her another glance, then returned his observation to the road ahead. "Don't you worry. After we make that list and I go find addresses on his friends you don't know, you'll have plenty to do. In the meantime, try to take a nap. Get caught up on some of that sleep you've missed. Maybe by tomorrow, I'll have enough info that the two of us can start following leads, together. Remember, you may have a long road ahead of you proving your innocence, and you need to be rested and ready for it."

"But I —"

"Listen, honey. You need to rest and then you need to give Marty some kind of heads-up as to what's going on. You need a clear head to say the right things to him. So please take my advice this time." He tried to give her an encouraging smile. "When do you have to go back to work?"

"Not for three more days."

Greg patted her clenched fists. "It will be okay. Maybe by that time, everything will already be cleared up. Let's hope for the best. Do you trust me, Sam?"

"You know I do," she said.

A small dimple appeared in his right cheek. "Then know you'll get through this. I promise."

Worrying her bottom lip, she realized he was right. She needed to tell her son what was going on. *But how? And what do I tell him? And how much should I tell him?*

There was no reason to upset Marty or make him worry if it turned out they didn't come after her. Her words needed to show strength and confidence, which she didn't have. If she let her fears seep out through her words or in her actions, Marty would latch on to them for himself. She didn't need to do that to him; he didn't need to sense fear. The scripture in Second Timothy about the Lord not giving man the spirit of fear but of power and of love and of a sound mind whispered in her spirit.

Hold on to that, girl, she told herself.

The car turned into the driveway but stopped suddenly, snatching her out of her deep thoughts. Blocking the car's path was another nondescript dark sedan.

"Not again!" she cried out.

Greg caught her by the elbow. "It'll be okay. Remember, we're prepared for them."

Her stomach twisted as she stared in disbelief. "I know we are, but not now." Her words tumbled from her mouth. "Not so soon. It's not fair."

Greg killed the motor. "Don't panic."

She tried to draw on his strength.

"Take a deep breath. Two of them, in fact; then release them slowly," he commanded.

Focusing her eyes on Greg, she did as she was told. Tears wanted to form, but she could not show weakness. She had to be strong, for Marty's sake, for her sake. *Fear is not from the Lord. Fear is from Satan. Don't grab hold of it. Breathe. Breathe. You have power. You have love. Power. Love. Power.* She breathed in and out with each word. Fast at first, but then down to a normal intake and exhale.

"That's better. Now remember: if they want to bring you in for questioning or even if they want to ask you questions here, you can't say a word without your attorney present. So let's walk in confidently and see what they have to say. They don't have a police car with them so it doesn't look like they're here to make an arrest. Most detectives, although they can and do make arrests, usually have an officer in a squad car with them to carry the prisoner back to the station when it's preplanned."

Sam's heartbeat went wild — double time, triple time. *So much for calming down.* How would she get through this? What was going to happen? She still hadn't told Marty anything. Would he come home to the detectives still here questioning her? Or to an empty house, and his mother in jail?

Lord, please don't let that happen. Please don't let them arrest me. Again she thought those words — *power* and *love.* The quick, shallow breaths she took with each word slowed as a veil of peace slid over her, and her heart rate returned to normal. *I can do all things through Christ who strengthens me.* The words *I will never leave you nor forsake you* touched her spirit as the calmness warmed her being.

Letting a tiny smile tinge her lips, she told Greg, "Okay. I'm ready."

He got out and hurried around the car to

open the door for her.

Sam turned in her seat as the door opened, ready to face her fate. She knew she was not alone.

Chapter 10

Margaret swung open the front door and came tearing down the steps. She reached Sam and Greg before they moved three steps from the car. "Ms. Sam, it's the same two men who came yesterday. They insisted I let them in. I'm so sorry."

Grabbing Margaret's hand, Sam gave it a squeeze, turned her around, and headed them all toward the house. "No problem, Margaret. It will all work out. I know you and Greg are here for me, too. We'll make it through." The three of them proceeded up the walk together, Greg bringing up the rear.

"Hello, gentlemen," Sam said as they stepped into the living room. Both detectives rose to their feet.

"Ms. Cain," they said in unison.

The lead detective took charge immediately. "We have a few more questions."

"Greg, these are the two detectives I was telling you about. Lieutenant Jones and

Sergeant Barnett." Sam pointed at each as she said their name and smiled as she spoke. She refused to let Jones intimidate her.

After acknowledging the introductions, Greg turned her way and gave her a slight nod with a half smile.

Suddenly she realized what his smile meant and said, "No problem, Lieutenant." Now was the time to do as Ms. Babineaux had instructed. "Just let me make a quick call to my lawyer before you begin your questions. I'd like her to be present this time when you ask me whatever you need."

"Why?" Jones stammered, apparently taken off guard. But then he swiftly added, "Do you need a lawyer? We're only asking for some more information. Or do you have something to hide?" He smirked. His eyes revealed that he didn't trust Sam. Clearly he was a cop who trusted no one, believed no one, and liked no one. A cop with a bad attitude.

Sam hadn't liked him from the time they'd met, and those feelings hadn't changed. He reminded her too much of her dead husband, the kind of abusive man who gave policemen a bad name.

The sergeant spoke in a more appealing tone as he said, "It's just a couple of follow-up questions, ma'am. Surely you don't need a lawyer for that." His eyes seemed genuine, but dare she chance it? She thought not.

Pulling the card Claire Babineaux had given her out of her purse she said, "I wish I didn't have to call one. But for my protection, I feel I must."

As she grabbed for the phone sitting on the end table next to the couch and started to lift it, Lieutenant Jones said, "Tell your lawyer to meet us at the station. We'll bring you in for questioning there." He moved toward her, pulling out his cuffs.

His scare tactics worked. Sam panicked and wanted to shout, "It's working," but didn't. Instead she pinned her eyes on Greg, hoping he had a way of slowing this man down. Did he have the right to force her downtown? And did he have to handcuff her? Sam pleaded silently with her eyes for Greg's help.

"Lieutenant, are you arresting her?" Greg stepped over, blocking Lieutenant Jones' path to Sam.

The detective cocked his head toward Greg, surveying him head to toe. "I wasn't planning on it, but it sounds like that's the way she wants it."

"I'll tell you what, Lieutenant. I'll bring Ms. Cain to headquarters. We'll call her attorney right now to meet us there. Since you aren't arresting her, there is no need for handcuffs, nor a need to ride with you to the station."

Jones' dark eyes smoldered as he continued to study Greg. With a sour look at his partner, he said, "Let's go. We'll ask our questions at the station."

Sam stood frozen, watching this entire scene unfold.

As Greg led the detectives outside, Margaret grabbed Sam's arm. "It's okay, honey. Call your lawyer. Greg is going to take care of you. I'll be here when Marty gets home. Don't you worry! He'll be fine. You'll be fine. Just hold your head up high, and remember you've done nothing wrong."

She's right. Do what you have to, Samantha Cain. You're not alone.

In almost robotic moves, Sam punched in the attorney's phone number. By the time Greg came back inside, Sam was ready to go with him. "Ms. Babineaux said she would meet us there."

Turning back to Margaret, she hugged her. "Thank you so much. I don't know what I would have done all these months without you, and you're still here helping me. One day I'll make it up to you."

"You've become family to me," Margaret

murmured, "so there's nothing to make up. I'm grateful to be a part of yours and Marty's lives."

Smiling at Margaret, Greg rested his hand gently on her shoulder. His eyes were thanking Margaret as his lips said, "Come on, Sam. Let's head down to the station and get this over with."

With friends like these two, how could she miss? She headed out the front door.

CHAPTER 11

The noise level and commotion as they stepped into the third precinct was so high, Sam almost couldn't hear herself think. Greg did the talking as they approached the main desk. Her gaze drifted around the room.

She didn't want to be there. Anywhere but there would have worked for her. Such horrid memories. First with Martin's suicide and the whole precinct believing Sam was responsible. Well, almost everyone. Then last year's hunt for the serial killer where she was the only living witness, which brought her to the station several times. The only good memory was her short time with Matthew. He did soften the hearts of most of the officers toward her, helping them see the truth. Sure, she knew there were good cops, but unfortunately the few bad cops like Martin and now Jones plagued her memory.

Let's get this over with. She concentrated on the officer speaking to Greg as he told them where to go. Homicide detectives had their own bullpen area, located on the second floor. Once they were there, a plainclothes detective led them to an interrogation room and told them to have a seat. The room was almost empty. It contained a table with a few chairs gathered around it. No light poured in from any window. It was a dim, depressing place with subdued overhead lighting.

Dread swept over Sam as a quiver of alarm sliced through her. She felt trapped, almost imprisoned, even before the door was shut. "This is not good. It's not good at all." Sam knew instantly if she couldn't take it in this small room she would never make it in prison. *Help me, Lord.*

"It'll be okay, Sam. Relax."

Pulling out a seat, she nodded and then lowered herself in the chair, trying to revive that sense of peace. Placing her hands on the table, she crossed one hand over the other, preventing the shakes.

"Trust me, Sam. It will be okay. They won't ask anything until your lawyer is present. And remember, I'm here with you." He patted her hand as the door swung open and slammed against the wall.

Her gaze shot over to the door. There, filling the empty space in the doorway, were the two homicide detectives. She focused on the lieutenant with an attitude. *Jones, what a creep! And what a way to make a grand entrance!* He was just a man, she reminded herself . . . a man with a badge. But she had done nothing wrong, so she need not worry.

Once all eyes were upon him, Lieutenant Jones marched to the table and plopped himself down, dropping a large file on the table as he sat. Sergeant Barnett followed him into the small room but seemed not as sure of himself as Jones. Or was it Jones he wasn't so sure of? Sam noticed the way the sergeant's green eyes studied the lieutenant.

Jones filled up what little space was left at the table in that small room as Barnett took the empty seat next to Jones but sat slightly away from the table. One lone chair sat in the corner by itself. Presumably, that would be pulled up to the table for her lawyer's benefit.

A knot formed in her throat but Sam forced it down as she glanced at Greg. He gave her a quick nod of assurance.

"While we wait on your lawyer," Jones said in a slow, dramatic melody, "I'll let you in on a little secret." He slapped the folder open on the table, then looked at Samantha with haughty eyes. The stiffened muscles on his face screamed of his smug, complacent attitude.

What kind of secret could he tell her? She wondered. There couldn't be more evidence against her. She hadn't done anything. Everything was circumstantial, so what possible secret could he have? And why would he share it with her if he were going to use it to take her down?

Jones whipped through the first several pages of his file folder. He stopped when he came to a stack of pictures, eight-by-tens. Sam watched as he picked up a handful of the pictures and dropped them one at a time in front of her — facing her — so that she saw all five very clearly.

A gasp slipped out as her eyes were drawn to the third picture laid out for display. Greg had shown her some of these at her own kitchen table, but this wasn't one of them. And at home she didn't feel as threatened.

In this picture, her boss lay out on the floor in his office, his eyes open in a dead stare. She wanted to cry out, "He can't be dead." But she didn't. She knew Ken was dead. Poor Dorothy. How would she get through all of this? Sam remembered not so long ago looking into the face of the man she loved, lying cold and dead on a gurney. She had made the positive ID for the medical examiner. Her heart broke for Dorothy having to go through the same thing.

Before Jones flipped over the next picture in his hand, Claire Babineaux strutted into the room. "I hope you haven't started questioning my client without my presence, Lieutenant Jones. Hello, Samantha and Greg." The woman stepped over to their side of the table. Greg rose instantly and pulled the empty chair next to Samantha. Claire sat down next to her client and laid her hand gently on top of Sam's. "We both know that's a no-no, Lieutenant."

Sam, cocooned between the two, felt her lawyer's strength flooding the room and Greg's protection penetrating deep into her emotions. She drew on both, feeling stronger almost immediately. Inhaling a deep breath, she pulled her eyes away from that horrid picture and looked at her lawyer. A slight smile touched her lips as she said, "Thanks for coming."

"And what are you showing my client? Crime scene photos? I thought you brought her here to ask questions. Do you have questions for my client, or was this one of your little scare tactics you use on innocent people?"

Jones grumbled under his breath as Barnett regarded Sam's lawyer with what almost appeared to be admiration.

"I was waiting on you, Claire. I didn't want to overstep my boundaries. Ms. Cain, does anything look out of the ordinary to you in these pictures?" He flashed his gaze on the lawyer as he said, "That is my first question. I assure you." He laid a couple more pictures over the first five he'd dropped in front of her. All were angles of her boss's office with the body lying in the midst of each shot.

"Do you mean, besides my boss laying there dead in the middle of the room?" Sam glared at the man. What a foolish question! Everything looked out of the ordinary when a dead man lay in the middle of it all.

"Of course, I mean besides your boss being dead. Take your time and look around the room. Do you see anything that should be there that isn't? Or anything that is there that shouldn't?" Jones glanced at his partner and flicked his brows as if to say, *Watch this. I've got her now.*

Sam's eyes flashed on her lawyer.

Claire nodded. "Go ahead. See if you notice anything out of the ordinary." Claire turned her eyes toward the detectives and added, "But let me remind you, Lieutenant, this isn't her office, so I'm sure she doesn't know everything in or about his office."

With an annoyed expression Jones demanded, barely moving his lips, "Just look at the pictures, Ms. Cain."

Quiet filled the room as Sam studied the photos one at a time. His fishing trophies all seemed to be displayed prominently on his credenza and his mounted fish hung on the walls. Papers were stacked in his in-box file, as well as his out-box file. The photos of his children and grandchildren stood angled on the bookcase. The high polish on his furniture seemed to be glowing as usual. Everything appeared to be in place.

After a few minutes passed, Sam raised her eyes and looked at the detective. "I don't see anything out of place. At least not to my knowledge," she added softly. "It looks like his office did the last time I was in it."

"You're sure? You don't see anything new?"

Sam skimmed over the photos one more time. "No. I'm sorry. I don't. It would probably be better if you asked Otto. He is in there more than anyone. He would know if anything was out of place. I so seldom go into Ken's office, working nights like I do."

Slapping another picture down on the

table, right on top of the other three she had been studying, he said, "How about now? Do you see anything out of the ordinary now? Look at this close-up shot of your boss's hand." He jabbed his thick finger at it as he tapped the picture over and over. "Tell me if what's in his hand belongs in his office."

This was the picture taken by the ME after he wrenched her boss's fingers open — a picture of her necklace. Her mouth grew dry. Her eyes flicked from the picture to Greg and then to Claire. *What do I say now? How do I answer this?* Her eyes begged her lawyer to step in and save the day. Obviously the police knew it was hers — not that she would deny it — but how did she tell the detective the necklace belonged to her?

"Ms. Cain. Do you recognize that necklace? Does it belong in his office?" The close-up of Ken's hand held a slim gold chain. On the chain was a heart encrusted in diamonds.

Claire again gave a slight nod. "Go ahead, Sam. Tell him."

She gulped, then said, "The necklace is mine." Pinning her eyes on the lieutenant, she said, "My fiancé gave it to me. I thought I'd misplaced it about a month or two ago somewhere in my home. I haven't been able to find it." Shaking her head, she added, "But I have no idea how it got in Ken's hand."

"You mean it didn't come off in a struggle between you and your boss the other night? You were the only one there. He was found dead after you left. He was clutching your necklace in his hand." His mouth twisted in a sneer. "Surely you can come up with a better excuse than 'I lost it.' "

Sam sat straight in her chair. "Lieutenant Jones, I'm not giving you excuses. I'm stating a fact. That necklace is very special to me. I only take it off at home, so I assumed it would show up sooner or later at my house." Lifting her pointer finger of her right hand and shaking it slightly, she said, "Not in the hand of my boss. I have no idea how it came to be there. But I guarantee not he nor anyone else snatched it off of my neck! That I would know."

Jones glared at her as Barnett sat quietly back. The smugness faded from Jones' face, and a slight smile edged the sergeant's lips. Not big, mind you, but enough for Sam to feel a little satisfaction creep into her joints. *Maybe the sergeant is on my side.*

"Is that all the questions you have for my client, Lieutenant? If so, we'll leave. If not, ask your questions."

"I have enough to arrest her right now. First, she didn't like her boss." Using his right hand he held down one of his fingers on his left hand. "It was a well-known fact in that office. Gives me *Motive.* Second, she was the only one there when he died. *Opportunity.*"

"Well, Lieutenant. You have circumstantial evidence at best. And I don't hear any means." Her lawyer rose. "I think we're through here."

Jones reached into his file, shuffled through a couple more pictures, then pulled one out and slapped it down on the table. "The letter opener that was found in the garbage but used to stab the victim in his chest had her prints on it." He stabbed his finger viciously in the air toward Samantha. Turning his gaze on Claire and holding up three fingers, waving them a little, he announced, "The third and final — *Means*!" The smugness returned.

"She already told you that was the dispatchers' letter opener that went missing. They all used it, so of course her prints would be on it," Greg said as a matter of fact.

Claire laid her hand gently on Greg's as she said, "Was it the murder weapon? Is that how he died, Lieutenant, from a stab wound? Even if so, it's still all circumstantial. Come on, Samantha, Greg, we're going."

Both stood to their feet, ready to follow Claire out of the room.

The detectives followed suit, but Jones threatened, "Ms. Cain, we *will* get more evidence. You will not get away with murder."

"But —" She turned to plead her innocence.

Claire interrupted. "She's innocent, Jones. Give it up. Come on, Sam. Let's get out of here."

Sam wanted to stay and defend herself to that wretched man, but Greg steered her out of the room and Claire followed. Once they made it out the front door, her lawyer looked at Sam. "You don't need to defend yourself. He needs to prove your guilt. Don't you worry. Just continue on with your life."

That would be great. Sam wished she could — and that the whole mess was behind her. Suddenly she heard the words of James 1:12 in her mind: *Blessed is the man who perseveres under trial, because having stood the test, that person will receive the crown of life that the Lord has promised to those who love him.* She knew she loved the

Lord; she just wished He didn't have so much faith in her to endure all these trials and tribulations. But she also knew the Lord loved her and would see her through.

One day at a time, she reminded herself.

CHAPTER 12

Opening the front door and about to step into her home, Sam heard a squeal and jumped, her nerves not quite under control these days.

"Momma!" Her son shot to his feet and scampered to the door. He wrapped his arms around her waist. "Momma. Are you okay? Is everything all right?"

Margaret rushed through the swinging door from the kitchen and mouthed, *I'm sorry.* She shrugged and raised her arms in a questioning motion as she continued lip talking. *I didn't know what to tell him.* Then she said aloud, "I explained to Marty that the detectives had a couple of questions they needed to ask you, but they needed to do it at the station for some reason. He was worried. I told him not to worry. You would be back soon. And here you are." She fixed an exaggerated smile on her face for Marty's sake.

Greg eased Sam and Marty into the living room so he could squeeze the rest of the way into the house and then closed the door behind him. "Why don't we go sit at the kitchen table and talk about it? I'm sure Marty would love to hear everything — if that's okay with you, Sam. Unless you want to speak to him in private."

"No. No. That would be great." She gave her son an extra tight hug. "We can all tell Marty what is going on with the police and why they've come to the house a couple of times."

Marty dropped his arms from around his mom and rushed past Margaret toward the kitchen. "Oh boy," he said as he pushed on the door. Even with his deep concern for his mother, the boy still embraced the excitement of a child when it came to cops and robbers. It was part fantasy for him, so she knew he didn't truly understand what was going on in the real world, even if he did know more reality than most kids his age should know. She hated having to tell him his mother was being accused of murder. *Not yet,* she reminded herself. But after all he'd been through, she hated telling him anything.

Margaret pulled three cups down from the cupboard and set them on the counter next to the coffee pot. "Coffee is fresh. Y'all had perfect timing," she said as she started pouring the hot black liquid in each cup.

"You are reading my mind, dear." Greg tossed a smile her way as he stepped closer to the countertop. "Thanks."

"Marty, would you like milk and cookies, or a soda?" Margaret asked, always thinking of everyone else.

"Mmm. Are the cookies homemade?" His innocent eyes rounded as they looked in anticipation.

"Sorry, sweetie. Store-bought."

His brow furrowed. After much consideration, he smacked his lips. "I guess that's still good. Thanks Ms. Margaret." He grinned as he scrambled into a chair at the table.

Sam watched the buzz in her kitchen as everyone did his own thing. When Greg finished fixing his cup of coffee and took a chair next to Marty, Sam slipped over and stood by Margaret. The dear woman poured two cups and started to add the cream and sugar for Sam. "Margaret," Sam whispered, "you don't have to wait on me all the time. You've become like family in the months you've been living with us. So please. Two things. Quit waiting on me hand and foot. And quit calling me Ms. Sam. Just call me

Sam. Okay?"

The curls on her head bounced as she nodded. "Thank you so much." She paused and then said, testing the waters, "Sam." Smiling, Margaret grabbed her black coffee and took the chair on the other side of Marty.

This left the chair straight across from Marty available for Sam. This way she was able to look straight into his eyes as she spoke, giving him the confidence that he needed to feel.

Sam stirred her coffee and joined them all at the table. *Lord, please give me the right words to say to Marty. He needs to know the truth but not so much that he becomes afraid.*

All eyes were upon her as she took a sip of her coffee and then set the cup on the table.

Marty took a bite of his Oreo cookie. As he crunched on the dark chocolate, he said, "I'm ready, Mom. Tell me. What's going on this time? I'm not going to have to go to Granny and Papaw's, am I?"

Poor child remembers the problems last year. "No, sweetheart." She smiled into his eyes. "Marty, do you remember my boss, Ken Richardson? You've met him before at some of the holiday gatherings at the terminal."

"Sure I remember him. He's that giant man." Marty peered up to the ceiling, waving his hands at the giant, and made a grunting noise as he exaggerated Ken's height slightly. "I've never seen anyone as tall as him." Marty took another bite of cookie and followed it with a gulp of cold milk.

Everyone couldn't help but smile at Marty's response. To a boy not quite four feet, a man over six feet tall would seem like a giant. "That's him, son. Well, something bad has happened to him. Someone killed Mr. Richardson."

His face grew solemn. "Oh no. Like Matthew?" His bottom lip began to quiver. "I'm sorry, Momma. I'm so sorry." He put his cookie down and dropped his head toward the tabletop. "I bet his kids miss him, too."

Sam didn't know about Greg and Margaret, but Marty's view on Ken's death choked her. It was all she could do to hold back the tears. He equated Ken's death to Matthew's death and how hard it had hit him. His little heart showed concern for Ken's kids — even though they were all adults now. How sweet. "I'm sure they do, sweetie. His wife, his kids, and his grandchildren are all going to miss him. It's a very sad thing."

"I'm sorry, Momma. Why do the police keep asking you questions?" He paused and then asked in a very small voice, "And why do people have to die?"

"The police think I might know something because he was found in his office early one morning and I had worked the night shift. In fact, they are hoping I know something — but unfortunately I don't." She reached out and grabbed her son's hand, holding it tight. "Baby, I wish I could give you a better answer on why people have to die, but it's just part of life. We live and we die. The important thing is how we live our life while we are alive."

"Like Matthew? He was a good guy. He loved helping people."

She fought back the tears. It was getting harder by the moment. Finally she said, "That's right, honey. He loved us and he loved others, always trying to help them."

Sam glanced at Margaret, whose eyes were rimmed with tears, and then to Greg, whose gaze was locked on Marty. She wished they would add a pearl of wisdom.

Lord, help me.

"And he loved the Lord. God is love, Marty. And Jesus tells us the most important thing for us to do is love others. Not just your friends, but even the people who are hard to love." She halted, believing the Lord Himself had prompted those words.

The boy looked up with bright eyes. "Do you love the man who killed Matthew, Momma?"

A heavy blow to the gut caught Sam off guard. She gasped as she tried to form the right words.

Greg stepped into the conversation, saving her. "Your momma loves everybody through Christ, Marty — even the bad man who killed Matthew. That was his job, to catch bad men and put them in prison so they couldn't hurt anyone. Unfortunately, this guy killed Matthew before he could arrest him. Your momma hates that the man killed Matthew, but she loves him through Christ and hopes that, during his time in prison, he finds the Lord."

Greg said it perfectly. *Thank You, Lord.*

Marty regarded Greg for several seconds, then finally said, "Okay. That makes sense." He bobbed his head up and down. Suddenly, his brows scrunched together and he peered sideways at Greg. With a slight hesitation he said, "And one day Momma will be happy again, right Uncle Greg?"

"You got it, buddy. One day." Greg lifted his hand for a high five, and Marty slapped it to him.

"All right." Marty snatched up his cookie and took another bite. "So, Ms. Margaret, what's for supper?"

Samantha sat back in her chair, unable to stop her amused grin. She watched as the three people she loved the most in the world rose from their chairs, seemingly content with the world. She loved her mom and dad as much, but they weren't there at the moment. Sam would catch them up on things in her life soon. Hopefully they would take it as well as Marty.

The three started moving around, all chattering with one another as they continued on into the living room. Oh, how she wished it were that simple.

One day, Lord, I will move on. But right now I still miss Matthew so much. Please let me hold on to him and my memories a little longer.

Her son appeared satisfied with the explanation she'd given him for what was going on as things in their lives were turned upside down again for the third time. If only she could explain it to the police simply enough to help them believe she had nothing to do with her boss's death. What should she do to clear her name? What could she do?

Wait on the Lord. He would direct her.

In the meantime, she needed to stay calm and safe in His arms.

CHAPTER 13

Two more days.

That thought crossed Sam's mind the minute she opened her eyes the next morning. Only two days left before she had to go back to work. Only two days left she could possibly use to help solve the mystery encircling her life. How could she use those days to help Greg turn the investigation away from her? On Sunday, she would return to work that evening, so she had better get busy!

After the big talk at the table with Marty yesterday afternoon, Sam sat down with a blank piece of paper and listed names of people she knew were friends of her boss. It wasn't a very long list, mind you, but it provided Greg with a starting point. He said he would begin the investigation right away and, as soon as he could, would bring her in on it. But she knew being around Greg in the beginning would only hinder the talks he planned with each of Ken's friends . . . especially if they knew she was the prime suspect, according to Detective Jones.

Of course, when Greg talked to TJ Roberts, the terminal manager Ken replaced, she could go with Greg. Sam didn't list him as a friend but as someone who may know something about Ken's reputation. She and TJ had gotten along well. Samantha had been his secretary and promoted to dispatcher on his watch. She hated it when the main office ran TJ off.

He stood up for his drivers. In fact, TJ went out of his way to take care of his people. That was what the main office didn't like about him . . . at least that was what she believed. And the customers loved TJ. They knew if he said he would do a job, it was going to be done. Some of those same customers only used her company as a backup now because they didn't trust Ken. They claimed he always billed them for more than they hauled, but no proof could be given. The tickets always matched what Ken said. Although the old customers didn't like it, they couldn't prove the weight tickets were wrong and that was what they were billed from.

She could also go with Greg to talk to Dean Smith, the present chief dispatcher.

He, too, wasn't a friend like the others listed. But since Ken made him chief dispatcher over guys with more seniority, everyone felt there was a special something about their relationship no one knew about but suspected. However, Dean did a fine job, and Sam had no complaints during the short time she was on days when he first started working for the company. Since she'd been nightshift dispatcher, she hadn't had much dealings with him but assumed he still did a good job. Like the boss, she only saw Dean at the dispatcher meetings. Sam felt certain he would talk freely around her. She would get with Greg this afternoon and see when he planned on talking with those two.

What can I do today? Maybe I should go pay my respects to Dorothy.

The funeral had been delayed since the ME hadn't released the body yet, but Sam knew for certain the woman already felt the loss and pain — just as she had felt when Matthew had been killed. It wasn't easy even now to go through each day. Thank God for Marty, giving her a reason every day to focus on him and live each day God blessed her with.

Dorothy and Ken's children were in their twenties and thirties. None lived at home anymore. Pity swept Sam's heart as she thought how lonely Dorothy's life had become overnight.

Sam slipped out of bed. Glancing at the clock she realized how early it was, so she pulled her hair up into a knot and clipped it. After taking a quick shower and dressing for the day, she made her bed and then padded down the hall to wake up Marty.

"Rise and shine, buddy. It's time to get up." She took a moment to observe her beautiful son's reaction as he moaned a little, then squirmed, twisting and turning under his bedsheets. Finally he grabbed his covers and dragged them over his head.

A small chuckle escaped her lips as she stepped over to his bed. "Come on, Marty." Leaning close, she whispered in a melodic tone, "It's Friday. The best day of the week. Get up, sleepy head." Slowly she eased his covers down, revealing his face one inch at a time. And then quickly she put her lips on his forehead, making a loud smooching sound, exaggerating the kisses.

"Aw, Mom!" The little boy wiped the sloppy kisses off his face and peeked open one eye. "I'll get up. Give me a few more minutes . . . please?"

She ruffled his reddish brown curls. "Okay, buddy. I'm going to go start a pot of coffee and then start mixing some pancake batter. If you get up and are dressed in time, you can have some for breakfast. If not, it will be a banana on the run for you. Don't sleep the morning away."

Smiling to herself, she left his door slightly ajar. If nothing else, the smell of bacon would bring him to his feet in a heartbeat. The boy loved bacon and pancakes. Tiptoeing down the hallway toward the kitchen, she paused at Margaret's bedroom and knocked softly on the door. In a quiet voice she said, "I'm putting on the coffee and then making pancakes if you want some." Sam didn't wait for an answer. She knew Margaret would come if she wanted to . . . or not. On Sam's off days, she made it a point of being the one who took care of Marty, so when Margaret joined them, it was like she was a part of the family. In the past few days she'd realized just how much Margaret felt like family to her. What a blessing!

Sam stood with her back to the kitchen table, stirring the batter while the dark brew dripped into the pot, filling the room with the aroma of the freshly roasted coffee. She savored the peace and quiet. With the mountain of worries that should concern her, she didn't dare ponder them. Sam had given them to Christ, and she didn't dare try to take them back — at least not at this moment. She hoped she'd left them with Him. Sam knew for a fact that He would lead her if she kept her faith in Him.

At the patter of little feet running into the kitchen, she pivoted and watched the whirlwind swoop up to the table. "So, my little man, you decided to come eat? Just in time. No banana on the run for you today."

He laughed out loud, dragged a chair from the table, and jumped up in the seat. "I wouldn't miss pancakes and bacon for anything in the world, Mom. You know it's my favorite." He rubbed his hands together. "And I'm ready to eat!"

Sam flipped his pancake and then grabbed the plate of bacon. Placing it on the table, she said, "Let's say a blessing. Your pancake is almost ready."

"Let me! Let me!" Enthusiasm bubbled over as he waved his hand in the air. She nodded so he began. "Dear Lord, thank You for my favorite breakfast. Bless it and the cook. Thank You for my mom who cooked it for me 'cause she loves me. Please, Lord, take care of her. In Jesus' name I pray. Amen."

"A-men." A voice from the hallway boomed out loud and strong, which was followed by Sam's "A-men." "I couldn't have said it better, young man." Margaret smiled at both Marty and Sam as she entered the room. "I'm ready for mine, too."

"Coming right up." Sam quickly poured more batter in the skillet and waited a couple of minutes. As the batter formed little circles, gelling the mixture, she knew when the pancake was ready for flipping.

While Margaret fixed a cup of coffee, Marty busied himself with spreading butter and watching it melt. Sticking a piece of bacon in his mouth he chomped down on it. "Um-um," he said, "this is so good. Thanks, Mom."

As swiftly as Sam scooped out the pancake and slapped it on a plate for Margaret, Sam wasted no time fixing her own and joining them at the table. There wasn't much talking going on this morning. It seemed everyone was too busy chewing.

When Marty took his last bite, he pushed his chair out and jumped to the floor. "Gonna go brush my teeth and then I'll be ready." As fast as the whirlwind rolled into the kitchen, it blew back out again.

"He is such a good boy." Margaret's voice oozed with pride. "You've done a wonderful job raising him."

"I hope I'm in it for the long haul . . .

raising him, I mean." Sam laid her fork down and picked up her glass of milk. Two swallows emptied the remains. Setting it down, she said, "I can't see God letting Marty suffer more than he already has."

"He has been through a lot, but the Lord saw him through it all. And He will continue to take care of Marty. Don't you worry."

Marty came running back into the kitchen with his school bag slung across his back.

"Looks like I finished just in time." Sam rose from her chair and hugged her son when he barreled his way into her.

"Breakfast was great, Mom. Thanks again." He hugged her waist and then kissed Margaret on the cheek. "See you this afternoon." And then Marty dashed toward the back door. "Come on, Mom. We don't want to be late."

"Coming, Son. I'm right behind you." She tapped Margaret gently on her shoulder as Sam passed. Snatching her keys off the hook in the kitchen and grabbing her purse off of the drain board, she reached for the back doorknob. "I'll be back in a few minutes," she said as she stepped outside.

In the car Marty chatted nonstop. "Today is going to be a great day, Mom. For me and for you. Don't you worry about a thing. I already prayed about it, and God told me not to worry. It's in His hands, and you know how big they are." The puffed out-cheeks shadowed his smile as he spoke with confidence.

What a wonderful son . . . and his faith.

To be so young, her son knew so much.

Thank You, Lord, she whispered in her head. She loved her little boy so much and would do anything for him. As fast as that thought came, she heard a quiet voice inside say, *"And you're My little girl. I'll do everything for you."* Sam's heart caught in her throat. *Out of the mouth of babes.* The comfort her son gave her was unexpected, yet so power-ful.

Turning into the horseshoe drive at school, she rolled slowly to a stop. As Marty opened the door to leap out, Sam said, "I love you, Son. Thanks for being my big man. You'll never know how much you mean to me."

"Aw, Mom." He flashed a smile at her and jumped out of the car.

Sam laughed to herself as she drove off.

She returned home to find the kitchen already cleaned to a sparkling shine and Margaret sitting at the kitchen table sipping on a cup of coffee. "Margaret, you shouldn't have. I'm off work for a couple more days. I can do these things, too, you know." She gave the woman's shoulder a squeeze, then grabbed the pot to pour herself another cup.

"Sit down and join me, would you, Sam? I have something I'd like to talk to you about, if it's okay." Margaret lifted her cup to her lips to take another sip, never taking her eyes off of Samantha.

"This sounds ominous." Sam sat at the table, not knowing what to think or how to take that statement. "Please tell me nothing happened while I was gone. Detective Jones didn't call the house or anything, I hope."

Margaret's soft curls bounced a little as she shook her head. "No. Nothing's happened, not today anyway." Seriousness filled her eyes. "Something did happen the other day, sort of. I need your advice . . . and ah . . . your opinion." Margaret's lips tightened into a fine line, and a slender line of concern formed between her brows.

"It will be okay, Margaret, whatever it is. I promise." Sam touched the older woman's hand. "What? Tell me all about it."

"Okay. Here goes." She took a deep breath. "Mr., ah . . ." She paused on his name and then smiled as she said sweetly, "*Greg* has been very friendly toward me lately."

"He likes you. So do we."

"I know that, but I don't mean like that."

Margaret held her hands up, palms facing out as if trying to stop every thought that might sidetrack her. "He sort of . . . flirted with me. I'm in my late fifties, so I'm not sure if he's just joking around and that's how he treats all women, or if he is truly flirting with *me.*" She pointed at herself. "The thing is, I like the man. When I met him months ago I thought he was hand-some. I've been a widow for so long and never before have I ever looked at a man and thought that." She stared into Sam's eyes like a little puppy, pleading for atten-tion. Only Margaret wanted guidance.

"Really?" Joy touched Sam's heart. She couldn't help but smile as she took another sip of her coffee. Putting the cup back down on the table, she lifted her left brow. "Sounds like maybe you have a crush on him. I mean, to notice him when you really haven't been finding any interest in any other man since your husband's passing. And to tell you the truth" — she paused, drawing Margaret's total attention even deeper — "I've been watching the two of you the past couple of days. I see the way he looks at you when you're skirting around the kitchen preparing dinner or breakfast, or whatever you're doing. I've seen the way you blush when he calls you 'dear.' I think it's so sweet. And I think maybe it's a two-sided interest."

A wide grin filled Margaret's face. Clasping her face in her hands, she whispered, "Truly?"

Sam gave a slight shrug. "I admit I've only known the man about a year, but from the way Matthew used to talk about him and what I've seen, he used to chase women all the time but never got serious with any. Ever. And in the last few years he quit chasing any and seemed to find contentment just living his life, such as it was. He even told Matthew how he regretted never finding that special woman he could love and settle down with. I believe that was the conversation that made Matthew realize he didn't want to wait any longer for letting his feelings for me be known. That was the night Matthew told me he had fallen in love with me. At the time we met, Matthew was a confirmed bachelor, believing he would never marry." She choked on those last words.

"I'm so sorry, Sam. I didn't mean to bring up such sad memories."

"My memories aren't sad. It's only the loss of him that's sad. The remembrances are wonderful." She relished the memories. "Matthew never married, and that was my fault. I put it off a bit too long. Don't make that mistake if Greg shows interest in you, and you are interested in him. You go for it, woman. You have a lot of life ahead of you. Live it."

"Oh, Sam, thank you." Margaret rose and hugged Sam.

After their shared embrace, Margaret backed away and apologized for taking up so much of her time.

"Don't be silly. I love that you felt open enough to share this with me. I love Greg, almost like a big brother, and I love you. What wouldn't be better than to see two people I love so much find they are perfect for one another? The only thing is, I'd hate to lose you . . . well, you know what I mean. You mean so much to Marty and take such good care of him."

"Let's not get carried away here. The man hasn't even asked me out or anything. Besides, you two are my new life, and I would never leave you. I love caring for Marty. He's come to be like a grandson I never had."

They laughed.

"Sorry. I tend to do that sometimes — think down the road a ways. By the way, I'm going to freshen up a bit and go pay my respects to Dorothy while Marty is at school. See if I can do anything for her. You know what I mean?"

"Do you think you should? What if the police have her believing you did it?"

Sam shook her head. "Surely Dorothy knows me better than that."

"She should. Well, be careful. I'm here if you need anything."

Sam grinned. "That's the thing I was talking about. You are always here for Marty and me. I'm spoiled."

"That won't change. Go do what you have to do."

On the drive to Dorothy's house those words Margaret said played over in Sam's mind. *What if the police have poisoned Dorothy's thoughts? Surely Dorothy wouldn't believe them. She's known me for several years.*

Sam paused before turning into their big horseshoe drive. Several cars were parked along the curb, so she pulled up behind the last one.

Maybe now wasn't a good time. It looked like others had the same idea, dropping by to pay their respects. Sam's heartbeat doubled as she opened the car door and stepped out.

"Give me the right words of encouragement for Dorothy through this time. Thank

You, Lord."

Climbing the few steps leading up to the front door, she held her head high, pressed the doorbell, and waited.

CHAPTER 14

The door opened wide, revealing a young woman dressed in a black silk button-down blouse tucked into black linen slacks. A few strands of blond hair fell loosely around her face. The rest was swept up, twisted, and secured on top of her head with two black shiny sticks stuck through the knot of hair. It was a stylish hairdo. Sam recognized Ken's oldest daughter immediately. "Dana. Hi," she said, extending her right hand. "I'd recognize you from your pictures anywhere. Your dad was very proud of all of you kids."

Dana slipped her hand into Sam's but gazed back with questioning eyes. Obviously, Sam wasn't as well known to Ken's children as they were to her.

Of course. That makes sense.

"Come in . . . please." The words spoken were almost robotic. Apparently they had already had a steady stream of visitors. The postponement of the funeral had to make things awkward for the family and friends.

"Pictures of you and your sisters and the grandkids cover his credenza and bookshelves in his office. Ken always spoke proudly of each of you. I've even met your two sisters at the crawfish boil last year. I don't believe you've come to any of our lunches at the terminal, though, so we've never met."

Releasing the grip of their hands, the young girl snatched hers back as if she'd been burned. Her eyes widened with recognition. Still blocking the entrance to Sam, Dana said, "You must be —"

"Samantha. Come in, dear. Dana, let her in." Dorothy sauntered over with both hands outstretched.

The daughter obeyed instantly, and Sam found herself in a warm embrace. Dorothy didn't listen to the police, obviously. She knew Sam was innocent. Relief flooded Sam's emotions.

Holding Dorothy in her arms, Sam whispered, "I am so sorry. I know how hard this is for you." Enhancing the hug, she tried to let her love surround the woman. Tears formed in Sam's eyes. She couldn't hold them back. Even though she didn't get along with Ken, her tears were for Dorothy and her loss. "I'm here for you if you need me, Dorothy. Anything."

The older woman squeezed Sam one quick time and then broke their contact. "Thank you, dear. Come with me. Meet some of our friends and family who came to pay their respects." Dorothy reached out her hand and Sam caught hold of it.

In the great room, so many people had gathered. Some were sitting, while others were gathered in groups. Sam recognized Susan and Cathy, the other two daughters of Ken and Dorothy, right away. Both girls turned their gaze upon Sam as she entered the room and then quickly looked away.

Sam gave herself a mental shake. *What is wrong with his girls? I understand they are upset, but why do all three of them act like I have done something to them?*

Reality struck. Apparently the chief detective on the case had shared his opinion with them, and they had chosen to believe it. *Maybe I shouldn't have come.* But at least Dorothy wasn't treating her poorly. Hopefully that meant Dorothy didn't believe Detective Jones' theory.

"Attention, everyone. This," Dorothy said as she placed her hand at the small of Sam's back and edged her forward, "is Ken's number one dispatcher."

Sam almost laughed out loud, but she

held it in. Why would Dorothy introduce her that way? Surely Ken had complained about Sam to Dorothy many times over the years. Maybe not. Oh well, she wasn't going to be the bearer of bad news to this woman. Maybe Ken didn't bring his bitterness home and poison his wife's opinion of her. Great.

Over the phone and on her occasional visits to the office, Dorothy had always been pleasant to Sam. Of course that was when Ken first started working for the company. He didn't wait long to stick her on the night shift.

Sam smiled timidly and nodded slightly to the group of people.

"I'm not going to call your names, but be sure and introduce yourself." Squeezing Sam at her waist, Dorothy said, "Ken probably told her stories about most of you. And some of you may have spoken with her on the phone when you called him at work. Introduce yourself to her as she makes her way around the room. Maybe she'll share a story or two from the terminal."

Scanning the faces from left to right, Sam knew no one. But the way Dorothy introduced her, Sam felt beholden to walk around the room and extend her condolences to each one. So as much as she didn't want to do it, she started on her left, with the oldest woman in the room. This was probably his mother. If so, Sam had spoken to her sometimes late at night when she had tried to reach Ken at home and got no answer. She figured Sam would know where he was. The sweet woman didn't want to disturb her son in the middle of anything important by calling his cell. She always checked with the people who worked for him, believing they knew his every move. The man never shared his private life with anyone . . . at least not with Sam.

On the nights his mom called, Sam could never tell her where he'd gone. She had paged him, leaving his mom's number as the call-back number. Whether he called her or not, Sam never knew but figured he had since Mrs. Richardson called her several times over the years for Sam to connect her to her son. The woman always took a few minutes out to share pleasantries, making Sam wonder how such a caring woman could raise such a hostile son.

The woman smiled brightly as she extended her trembling hand. "Oh, how wonderful to finally meet you in person, dear. Your smile always came across the line when I spoke to you on the phone. I thank you for always being willing to help me get in touch with my son."

Sam took the wrinkled but soft hand and covered it with her own. "Mrs. Richardson, it was always a pleasure talking with you. I'm sorry we're meeting under such sad circumstances."

Mrs. Richardson's eyes rimmed with tears as they chatted. The older woman's hands quivered as they held tightly to Sam's.

"Your son loved you very much. He told us tales of his youth, and how he gave you a lot of grief. He also told us how you always whipped him in line." Sam hoped those words gave the woman some comfort.

A tear slipped down her cheek, and she sniffed. "Thank you, dear. Thank you so much." Mrs. Richardson inhaled a quick gasp. "Your children aren't supposed to die before you. No parent should have to bury her child, no matter how old. It's not fair." Tears began to fall in a steady stream.

Sam knelt before the older woman and whispered words of comfort. As the sobs slowed down and tears dried, Sam rose to her feet. "Take care, Mrs. Richardson. One day at a time the Lord will see you through."

"Thanks, dear." She touched the tissue under her eyes one more time.

Sam bade her good-bye and moved on to the next group of people. She didn't stay as long there as she had with Ken's mom. In fact, with each group she made her stay shorter and shorter. As much as she wanted to be there for Dorothy, she had no intention of getting to know Ken's family and friends in one swift walk around the room.

All three daughters hovered around Dorothy, almost like a shield. Her earlier thoughts had to be true. They had to have heard the talk from the detectives. All three regarded her with condemnation — all but Dorothy. Drawing a deep breath, she strode over to the group to say good-bye.

Before she could, the middle daughter, Susan, stepped out of the group, blocking Sam's way. "You've got nerve." Her voice, though whispered so others weren't aware of the evil tone, stopped Sam cold.

She swallowed a lump in her throat. *Help me, Lord.*

"I'm sorry, Susan. I'm here to pay my respects to you and your mom. I'm not ashamed of anything. Please let me say good-bye to your mother, and I'll be on my way."

Susan stood firm and tall, towering over Sam's five-foot, one-inch frame. As the daughter's eyes shot daggers and her mouth opened to fire more words at Sam, Dorothy caught her daughter by the elbow. "Susan, sweetheart, go see if Grandma wants another cup of coffee."

"Mother," she said strongly, trying to tug free as she pleaded.

"Go. Now. Everything is fine." Dorothy released her daughter's arm and the girl stepped away. Extending her hand, Dorothy said, "I'm sorry. Emotions are a little tense around here. These girls don't seem to know what to do with their grief."

Sam wanted to deny Susan's allegations, or at least her insinuations, but decided now wasn't the time. Dorothy knew Sam would never hurt her husband, even if she could have. It wasn't in Sam's nature to hurt anyone. Grasping Dorothy's outstretched hand, Sam stated, "I'm truly sorry for your loss. I'm still grieving over my loss of Matthew, so I do know how you feel. Again, if I can do *anything* for you, let me know."

The elegant woman squeezed Sam's hand. "I will, dear. Thank you for coming and sharing your heart with my family and me. We appreciate it very much." Dorothy dropped Sam's hand and placed her hand at the small of Sam's back as she directed her toward the front door.

Did Dorothy want her out of there, too? Did she blame Sam for her husband's death? Oh, how Sam hoped not.

Driving home, Sam prayed for the Lord

to comfort the family. She reminded herself that everyone grieves in their own way. The kids needed someone to blame, and she seemed to be an easy target. But Sam knew the truth. She had not done a thing. The only thing she wished was she had heard the scuffle upstairs that led to his death, so she could have prevented it. But she hadn't, and she couldn't change the past.

Help us, Lord, to find the truth. Lead Greg in the right direction since the police seem to have fixated on my guilt.

Where to go now? What was the next step? She knew she had to trust the Lord to prove her innocence. If there was anything He needed her to do, He'd let her know. In the meantime she would go wherever she felt His leading.

Waiting was the hardest part. But that was the next step. Maybe Greg would have something for her to do when she got home. Sam pressed the accelerator in expectation as the car rolled a little faster down the road.

CHAPTER 15

Detective Barnett couldn't understand why Jones, the lead detective, was so convinced that Samantha Cain killed her boss. Jones' misconception had Mark baffled. How could he even think such a thing? She was so small, and her boss was so big. Sure, little people kill big people all the time, but usually signs of a struggle would be present. Or in some cases the ME would find drugs in the bloodstream, giving reason why the smaller person could bring down the larger one without using much force. Neither held true in this instance . . . at least not in the preliminary report. There wasn't even blood spatter around the room showing an attack with the letter opener. One solid hit . . . and very little spatter. Maybe the drug had been undetected in the first test, and Richardson lay still on the floor as Cain slammed the knife in his chest, piercing the lung and causing asphyxiation. That was the only thing that made sense at the present. If Jones was correct, maybe Samantha Cain had sedated him in some form that the ME had not uncovered yet.

Detectives couldn't solve cases merely on conjecture, though. They had to study all the facts, all the evidence. The evidence they'd collected spoke clearly to Mark. Not clear enough to exonerate Samantha Cain, but clear enough to know Jones was headed in the wrong direction. To the young sergeant, it was plain someone was setting Ms. Cain up. No one in their right mind would kill someone where they would be the only suspect. Everything was circumstantial and too obvious at that.

The office was found with only a small pool of blood around the wound and very little spatter, so his heart was still beating when stabbed, but Richardson didn't fight back. The thrust penetrating his body had not been substantial. The room itself was found clean and neat. No overturned furniture. Not even papers out of place. That ruled out a struggle for sure. Mark felt there was a chance the body had been placed there.

But still it didn't explain why Samantha Cain didn't hear or see anyone that night. How could that have happened?

A toxicology report would come in sometime today. Maybe that would clear up some things, but no matter how he looked at this case, read the evidence, or listened to the people interviewed, in his gut Mark could not believe this little woman killed anyone, especially a man of Ken Richardson's stature.

Across the desks, Jones was munching on doughnuts and slurping down coffee. Mark lowered his gaze to the folder in front of him. There had to be more to the man's death than merely a disgruntled employee. They needed to push his friends and coworkers harder, even check more into his family life. Everyone painted this man as a saint — everyone except some of his employees. Others made it sound like he was their best friend. Probably trying to look good for the next boss. There had to be more, and it was his and Jones' job to find it.

Frustrated, he rubbed his clean-shaven face and pulled his keyboard over in front of him. There were other ways to find out things about people in today's world, the world of the Internet.

Tapping the keyboard, he filled the search bar with Richardson's full name. In seconds over ten hits appeared. There were too many for his liking, but Mark scanned the various links. Speed-reading the text, he found a lawyer, a doctor, and eight other professionals on one link all living in New York City, another man in Georgia, and someone's link on Facebook with no personal profile included.

"Aha," Mark whispered as his fingers went back up to Google and typed in Facebook. There were so many social media networks for him to search; he was bound to find something else on the victim . . . using the computer. Today some of the older generation hadn't caught on to using high-tech gadgets. To people like Jones, it was a bother to have to use the computer. That was one of the reasons Jones liked having Mark as his partner — he keyed in all their reports. The only thing Ben Jones did on the computer was read his e-mails and play games. Nothing too technical, of course.

Forty-five minutes later, Mark found a lead. On one of the networks Richardson had a page. It didn't look condemning on the surface, but some of the typed chatter, the wording patterns, led Mark to believe there was more behind the innocent conversations the victim had with his social media pals. Don't people realize anyone could find them if they thought to look?

And once their words, pictures, or videos were in the airwaves, there was no taking them back.

After copying and pasting several postings, he would see if one of their computer geeks could crack the code, as well as figure out to whom the IP addresses Richardson communicated with belonged.

As his list printed, another thought surfaced — texts on the victim's phone. Sure, they didn't find anything incriminating on the phone calls or the texts left in full view for anyone looking at the vic's phone, now in evidence lockup. But when the customer deleted a message, the phone company still had a record of that message. He would get a warrant and then secure a copy of the last six months of texts to and from the victim. Maybe someone other than the obvious disgruntled worker had threatened Mr. Richardson — and maybe he would find out more about the man's life . . . something suspicious.

Mark scanned the printed page of what he had saved and then folded it, sticking it in his back pocket. Picking up the phone, he started to call Kevin from IT but realized he didn't want Jones to hear him. Instead he sent an e-mail requesting Kevin to check out what he had copied and pasted, as well as the victim's social media page, and see if he could determine if there was a hidden code. At least the man could trace the messages back to IP addresses and try to locate the true names and addresses for him so Mark could speak one-on-one with each of them.

An hour and a half had passed and his partner hadn't said a word to him. Mark wondered what Jones was doing at his desk. Surely he'd finished his breakfast by now. Glancing over, he found his partner reading over something on his computer. Maybe the old man got wise and decided to do a little digging himself.

Negative. Jones was probably reading his e-mails. That was the majority of the old man's Internet knowledge.

"Hey, Ben, I think I found us another possible lead," Mark said across their desks. They faced each other, making it easier for the two as partners to communicate to one another as they discussed a case they were working on.

Jones stuck his left hand up in the air with one finger sticking out, never taking his eyes off the computer screen, as if to say, *Wait one minute. I'm in the middle of something.*

Mark clamped his mouth shut against the words he wanted to say. Why didn't Jones want to know whom else could possibly be blamed? That remark should have gotten his partner's full attention, but he was so fixated on bringing Samantha Cain down, he probably didn't even want to hear what Mark had to say.

"We got her!" Jones slammed his hands together with one loud clap and then jumped to his feet, almost dancing a jig as he stomped around bobbing his neck back and forth and pumping the air with his fists, like he'd just scored a touchdown.

Shaking his head, Mark said, his voice growing louder with each word, "Ben, did you not hear what I said when you told me to wait? I said I found another lead."

Jones stopped his dancing and frowned in Mark's direction. "What's with you, partner? You've been so fixated from the beginning that it wasn't Ms. Cain. Why, when it's so obvious she did it?" He stood motionless, staring at his partner in disbelief.

Trying to keep calm, Mark sat back in his chair.

Enough! Slapping his hands to the arms of his chair, he stood in disgust and aggravation. With his eyes penetrating, burning a hole through Jones', Mark said in a harsh voice, "And why is it you've already tried and convicted Ms. Cain? You've got some stick —"

"That's enough, Barnett," Jones interrupted. "Let's roll. You young people will never learn." He grabbed his crumpled suit jacket off the back of his chair and stepped to the printer. Pulling a piece of paper off the machine, he folded it and stuck it in his breast pocket. "I'm the lead detective, and I've got a new piece of evidence. One that explains how that little woman did the dirty deed. Even you'll have to believe it."

I doubt it, Mark thought but knew better than to speak aloud. The sneer on his partner's face caused Mark's stomach to churn. What was his problem?

Getting irrefutable evidence would be the only way to change Ben's mind. And he would do it. Mark would follow his own lead on his own time without sharing his findings with Jones, until he could tie it up in a bow, so to speak. Mark hoped he found facts to back up his possible theory soon. Then he'd clue Jones in. The man didn't really want to hear anything that would exonerate Ms. Cain. So Mark would keep it to himself for the time being.

Right now he wanted to refuse to go with the detective, but he couldn't. Ben Jones was the lead on this and every case they worked together. Mark may have to follow Detective Jones, but he didn't have to agree with the man. He would go so he could keep himself abreast of what Jones was plotting against Samantha Cain. Maybe that was the best way to handle this case, this time. He hated going behind his partner's back, but what choice did he have?

"We're going to slip by the DA's office and get a warrant to search Samantha Cain's home. If my gut is right, we'll find all the evidence we need."

Mark grabbed his suit coat and followed Jones to the elevator.

We'll see.

CHAPTER 16

Sam saw Greg's black Accord parked at the curb of her house when she turned into the driveway. She hoped he had good news. After that visit to the Richardsons' home, she could use a little uplifting.

Parked around back, she killed the motor and stepped out of her Toyota. By the time she walked over to the back steps, she heard laughter from the kitchen. Greg must be telling one of his many stories. She was glad Margaret found things to smile about again. When the woman first came to work for them, she'd maintained a serious countenance. After a few months, Marty had her smiling most of the time. Matthew occasionally made her laugh, but never a full belly laugh. That was Greg's doing, and it sounded wonderful. He'd even worked hard to make Sam at least smile since Matthew's death.

He'd been successful — until now.

Unfortunately now her mind stayed too busy to laugh. Too busy to smile. She tried not to worry because she'd given her problems to the Lord, but she couldn't help but ponder the situation. *I guess the spirit is willing but the body is weak.*

Sticking the key in the knob, she unlocked the door and then opened it. The aroma of onions and garlic simmering on the stove assaulted her senses the minute she stepped inside. "Um, um, um. Something smells delicious in here. What are you cooking?"

"Steak and gravy. I hope that's okay by you."

Greg's chest puffed up slightly. "It's my favorite. She said there was enough for me, too. Hope you don't mind, but I'll be joining you all for supper." Greg glanced at Sam, smiling as he spoke, but when his gaze turned to Margaret, his smile deepened. If Sam wasn't seeing things, she believed Greg's eyes even twinkled.

"Sounds good to me — supper and you're staying. The smell sure has my stomach calling out." Dropping her purse and keys in their usual spot on the counter, she pulled a cup out of the cupboard.

"Would you like me to fix you a snack? Dinner is a few hours away. Knowing you, you didn't bother to grab lunch while you were out today, did you?" Margaret knew her so well.

With a slight chuckle, Sam said, "Don't mother-hen me, Margaret, but you're right. I didn't eat lunch. I —"

"Oh. That reminds me." Turning on her heel, Margaret announced, "Your mom called and she wants you to call her back. I can't believe I almost forgot to tell you."

"You didn't tell her anything, did you?"

"Of course not."

A sigh of relief escaped Sam's lips as she set the cup on the counter.

"It's not my place," Margaret said, her eyes flitting from Sam to Greg and back again to Sam. It was like a neon sign flashing *Guilty* over and over.

So did she tell her parents anything? Sam wasn't sure. "Margaret?" she questioned softly. "What are you hiding? Or what did you say?" Sam knew that look on Margaret's face meant something.

The older woman raised her brows. "I promise I didn't say anything to your parents." Dropping her gaze to the floor, she whispered, "But . . ."

"Out with it, woman."

"Oh my," Margaret murmured. She tapped her fingertips to her lips. Pausing for another second or two, she glanced again at

Greg for what appeared to be direction or a spot of encouragement. He gave her a supportive nod and the woman continued. "But I was just telling Greg that I thought you needed to share this with them. I know you don't want to worry your parents, but they want to be there for you. I think if they find out another way, it would hurt them deeply. They love you so much, Sam."

Sam gathered her long strands of hair into a form of ponytail, dropping it over her left shoulder. The longer her hair got, the more she routinely repeated this action. Her anxious fingers continued to play with her long strands as she thought. Finally, she nodded. "You're right. I'll call them now."

Sam slipped to the bedroom to make the call. She wanted a little privacy because she had no idea how her mother or father would react. Besides, Marty didn't need to hear the worry that would probably pour from her voice. Glancing at her watch, she saw she had over an hour before the bus dropped him off in front of the house.

Her mother answered on the second ring. "Hello." Her parents still lived the old way, no caller ID or anything to tell them in advance who was on the other end of the line.

"Hey, Momma. It's me."

"Oh, sweetheart. I knew it. I knew it. I hear it in your voice. I told your father Margaret sounded upset even though she tried to hide it. What can we do? And what is going on? Please tell me you're okay — and Marty. Dear, don't keep us in the dark." She called in the background, "Honey, it's Samantha. Come quick."

"We're okay, Momma, but something is going on. But I don't want you or Dad to be upset. Tell Dad everything is okay."

"One second. He'll be here in a moment."

Sam could see her mother's gaze in her mind's eye, flitting back and forth from the phone to the doorway, anticipating her dad's arrival. She waited in silence as she imagined her mother's every move.

"Okay, dear. He's here. Go ahead and tell us."

Sam knew they both put their ears up next to the phone, waiting to hear what Sam had to say. A smile touched her lips. She loved them so much. "First let me say, everything is okay. The sad thing is my boss was killed the other day, and they found him in his office early the next morning. Unfortunately I was the one who worked the night shift before the body was found, and I seem to be the police's number one suspect."

Her mother, Diane, had drawn in a deep

breath when she heard about Ken Richardson's death, but when she heard the police suspected Sam, a squeal escaped.

"It's okay, Mom. I didn't do it. Greg is helping me find proof since the police . . . well, not all of them." She didn't want to paint the wrong picture for her mother. "There is one detective who seems to believe in my innocence. Or, more to the point, he doesn't seem as strong as his partner in thinking I'm the guilty party."

"Hold on, Sam," her father said.

Her father didn't give her a choice. She heard the clank of the phone hit the counter and then the dragging of a chair on the floor. Sam wished she could see in their kitchen and know what was going on. "Dad. Daddy, can you hear me? What's happening?"

"Samantha, it's okay. Your mom needed to sit down for a minute. This is a little much. How can the police think a person as sweet as you could possibly kill your boss — even if he is a monster to you?"

"I don't know, Daddy, but I do know everything will be okay. I know God is taking care of things and He's surrounding me with people to help me and Marty."

"Well baby girl, keep us posted," her dad said. "And if we can do anything, let us know. Marty can come stay with us again. Anytime. You know we'd love to have him."

"I do. Thanks, Daddy. Give Momma a hug for me, and you two don't worry. Before, Marty's life could have been in danger. That isn't the problem this time, so I'd rather not interrupt his schooling. Margaret is here for him every day when I'm not. We're keeping him in the loop but not by telling him everything. He's almost nine now. I can't treat him like a baby. And you'd be so proud of him."

"We are, dear. We'll be praying for you both. Take care. We love you. Give our love to Marty."

Sam said her good-byes and they hung up. She glanced at her watch and hurried to the kitchen. They needed to talk before Marty got home. She wanted to tell them what happened when she visited Dorothy's home without Marty hearing the details. Sure, she had shared the circumstances of what was going on to a degree with her son, but there was no need for him to hear everything.

After pouring a cup of coffee, Sam added cream and sugar and then joined Margaret and Greg at the kitchen table. "Margaret, you can rest your mind now. Mom and Dad know everything. Thanks for suggesting I call." She quickly updated them both on her visit to the Richardsons' home, paying her respects.

Margaret shook her head in sorrow.

Greg said, "You probably shouldn't have gone there, but at least you've let them see you're not afraid. Maybe that alone will be enough to have Mrs. Richardson suggest the police check other avenues. I'm sure they talked to her a good bit in the beginning of the investigation, trying to find out all they could about her husband. Well, we hope they did, anyway."

She agreed with him. "Now, Greg, did you find out anything today that might help divert the investigation away from me?"

"Turns out your perfect boss had a couple of flaws." He gave Sam a half smile.

A moan of expectation burbled up from deep within. Her heart expanded as it filled with hope for the truth. "Really? Great! Tell me more."

"He likes to gamble and chase women."

"Wow," Sam said, shocked. "That I wouldn't have guessed in a million years. I knew he wasn't perfect, but I truly thought he was faithful to Dorothy. And the way he takes care of his family, even though they've all grown and left the house, the man is . . . *was* . . . very generous, almost to a fault."

"That's something else I need to look at closer. Thanks."

Sam raised a brow in question.

"The kids and their dependency on him. Parents do some crazy things when it comes to their kids. Helping them out of trouble, which only allows them to make bigger mistakes, and then assuming Daddy will bail them out again . . . that could lead to some powerful enemies, if you know what I mean." He shrugged. "I want to cover all bases."

Queasiness gnawed at her stomach. Sam hated that she and Greg were digging into Ken's past and his family affairs. It seemed too personal to her.

"Don't fret, little lady. This is your life we're talking about. And if it takes opening some of their closet doors to expose other possibilities, then that is what we'll do. Right?"

Sam sat in silence, thinking what an awful thing they had to do.

When Sam didn't speak up, Margaret did. "Right. Besides, if the man's a gambler, he may have a few enemies who would want to kill him. So don't you worry! Greg will get the police looking in the right direction." The woman stepped over to the coffee-maker. After refilling her cup, she offered more to Greg.

"Thanks, Babe, I don't mind if I do." He held his cup up so she could pour more in the empty mug.

"Sam?" Margaret turned the pot in her direction. After a slight nod, Margaret topped off Sam's cup and then grabbed the sugar bowl and cream pitcher, moving them to the table.

While everyone tended to his or her coffee, a thought emerged. *Didn't bookies like gamblers? That was how they made their money.* And as much money as Ken seemed to have, she doubted he owed anything to them. Sam felt certain he paid all of his debts. "So how will this help? Surely if Ken gambled, he won more than he lost. And when he lost, I'm sure he paid what he owed. The man was loaded and making great money. Sometimes we, his employees, believed he even made a few deals under the table, if you know what I mean."

"Nobody wins all the time," Greg assured her. "And the man may not —"

A loud pounding on the front door interrupted his words.

Rolling her eyes, Sam rose to her feet. "It's them again. I know it. They never ring the doorbell. It's like pounding on the door is more powerful. And that big detective loves pushing his power."

"Let me get it." Greg headed toward the living room.

"No," she said, stopping him in his tracks. "I don't want them to think I'm afraid, 'cause I'm not. This will work out in the end. I just have to be strong. You two stay in here. I'll call you if I need you."

"If you're sure." Greg stepped back.

Margaret's gaze darted from the direction of the front room to the stove. Making a snap decision, she stepped over to where the steaks were stewing in the gravy and turned the knob. Instantly the fire went off from under the pot.

"Good idea. Thanks. I'd hate for them to burn our supper, too." Sam pushed through the swinging door. As she moved toward the front door, she glanced through the big picture window and called out in a hushed tone, "I guess you better come on in here after all, Greg. They brought police cars with them." Although she had planned to be strong, her cracking voice revealed a smidgen of fear. The backup troops with the detectives could be the cause of that. She knew what it meant. Trouble. It looked like they were here to arrest her. But why so many cars?

As she opened the front door, Greg and

Margaret rushed through the swinging door and then stood back. They were there if she needed them but not hovering so the detectives could see her strength.

"Well, well, if it isn't my two favorite detectives! And look, they brought some friends with them." She kept her tone sweet until her eyes met the convicting ones of Detective Ben Jones.

"What do you want now?" she asked without pushing open the screened door. Sam didn't want to invite them into her home again. Although she hadn't meant to be disrespectful, she was getting tired of the smugness on that man's face. Her annoyance spilled into her words.

Holding a paper up, Jones opened the screen door. "Step aside," he said in an authoritative manner. "We have a warrant to search your premises."

"For what?" She backed up, allowing him entrance as she took the paper. "I don't understand. What are you looking for here at my house?"

"It's on the warrant. I suggest you read it."

"I'll call Claire." Greg whipped out his cell from his pocket and started dialing.

Fighting tears, Sam murmured, "This can't be happening to me. Not again."

Inside she screamed, *Why, Lord? Why me? Why so much? I know You don't give us any more than we can handle, but I think You just believe a little too much in me. Stop this insanity . . . please.*

Margaret rapidly moved to Sam's side. "It'll be okay. Hang in there." Her hands enveloped Sam's forearms, pouring courage and strength into her veins.

Sam surveyed the other detective as he stepped through the door. An expression of what appeared to be regret flashed in his eyes. Was he regretting or apologizing for the intrusion? Or was he apologizing for his partner? Either was greatly accepted and soothed her frustration slightly.

The men dressed in uniform followed the detectives and immediately dispersed in every direction. As they scattered, Greg hung up his phone. "Claire's on her way. She said just stand back and don't say a word."

Sam sighed. *Wait. Of course.*

What else could she do?

CHAPTER 17

"If you three will take a seat and stay out of our way, we should be out of here soon." Jones wasn't asking. He was telling. "Detective. Stay here with them. I'll go see what the men are finding." His partner gave a nod as he stood with his back to the wall and his arms folded across his chest.

Sam wasn't sure if she could talk to him or not. Her lawyer had said to wait for her. But surely that didn't include being impolite to the one man she thought might be on her side — Jones' partner. He never looked in a negative way at Sam. He always seemed to be the one who tried to help her see that he and his partner were only doing their job.

Sighing, she decided to be herself. "Detective Barnett, is it?"

He nodded and revealed a partial smile.

"Can I get you a cup of coffee?"

"Thanks, but no thanks, ma'am. We'll be

through here in a short time. Sorry for the intrusion."

"Tell me, Barnett," Greg said, as he looked the detective up and down. "You don't seem as pushed to lock up Samantha Cain as your partner. What is it with that man? Why is he out to get Sam instead of doing his job and searching all the possibilities?" Greg stepped closer to the detective.

"And you are?"

"I'm Greg Singleton. Retired from the force five years ago. I was Detective Singleton, with Homicide, for over twenty years." He extended his hand, and Barnett returned the greeting. "I was partner to Matthew Jefferies' dad. Did you know Matthew Jefferies? He was Samantha's fiancé."

"I knew of him, sir. And," glancing at Samantha, he added, "I knew Ms. Cain was engaged to him before his death. Sorry, ma'am."

Samantha and Margaret both watched as the two exchanged words. When the detective acknowledged Sam, giving her his sympathies, a chord touched her heartstrings.

"Like I said, it's been awhile since I've been with the force, but I'm sure police procedure is still the same. Follow the evidence. Her necklace in her boss's hand

184

— everyone knows was planted. If she had wanted to kill him, surely she wouldn't be dumb enough to kill him where she would be your first and only suspect. Give the woman a little credit."

The detective raised his brows and glanced toward the two doors exiting the living room leading to other parts of the house. Then he said quickly, almost as if he didn't want to be overheard, "I understand you completely, sir. We —" He cleared his throat. "We are looking into all the evidence, sir, ma'am. You can count on it." His gaze slipped from Greg to Samantha as his eyes revealed sincerity.

The doorbell chimed and Sam looked to the detective for permission to answer the door. He gave her a nod, letting her know she could. Opening the door, Sam said, "Oh, Ms. Babineaux, thank you for coming so quickly."

Greg stepped beside them and handed her the warrant. Greg could have scanned it, but Sam felt sure he was more at ease letting someone in the legal world be certain of its contents.

Claire's gaze skimmed over the papers and then said, "This warrant entitles them to look throughout your home and storage and any buildings on the premises, as well as your car."

"What are they looking for?"

"According to this warrant, Ken Richardson was not killed by that single stab to the chest that they thought in the preliminary report had penetrated the lung. Their finding now states death by poison."

Margaret jumped to her feet. "So they're looking for poisons? Oh, no." Her gaze jumped from one person to the other. Then, as fast as she'd said it, she looked like she wished she could have pulled the words back into her mouth.

But everything happened for a reason. Sam knew if they had poison around the house, it was for a good reason, and it wasn't to kill anyone. Greg stood and slipped over to Margaret's side. He seemed to give her comfort as he hugged her, and then helped her back onto the sofa. He squeezed in next to her. Sam heard him whispering, "It'll be okay. Don't worry. Relax. What are you thinking that's upsetting you so?"

The lawyer stared in Margaret's direction, never letting her eyes waver. Finally Claire said, "Yes. That is exactly what they are looking for. So what is it that's upsetting you so, ma'am? And who are you?"

"That's Margaret. She lives with us. She

186

takes care of my son and me. She's almost like family." Sam tried to assure Margaret as well as Claire Babineaux.

Margaret reached out to Sam. "I'm so sorry." Avoiding the detective's glare, she turned her eyes on the attorney. "We have rat poison in the shed out back. I know, because I bought it. Ms. Cain is not even aware of it. At least I don't remember ever telling her." She shivered. "I'm so sorry," she whispered again as she eyed Samantha with a soul-wrenching look.

Sam stared at her friend. "My heavens. Poison? What on earth for? We don't have any rats, do we?"

"As a matter of fact, we did, but we don't anymore," Margaret explained. "One night, while you were working, I heard skittering across the ceiling. Years ago we had rats in the attic, and I remembered the sound all too well. So I went to the hardware store the next day and purchased a large bag of rat poison pellets and scattered them up in the attic."

"I don't remember ever smelling a dead rat," Sam said slowly. "I know when we've killed them at work with poison, the stench is deadly when those things crawl into the wall somewhere and die. That's a smell you don't forget."

"I know what you mean. But the kind of poison I bought was supposed to make them run away and find water. It makes them thirsty. And living across from the lake, I felt sure they'd run across the road and crawl into the lake and die. Never heard them again, so I believed it worked. Anyway, because there's a small child in the home, I felt led to put the remainder of the package of pellets outside in the storeroom under lock and key. I didn't want Marty to accidentally find it and there be a horrible mishap."

Sam moved over to the couch and wrapped her arms around Margaret. After giving her a hug, she released her and looked into her eyes. "You are the best. Thank you."

"I hope you're not in trouble for something I did," Margaret said.

"It'll be okay. Don't you worry!"

"The ME's report indicated the type of poison. Rat poison wasn't the killing aid. It was potassium cyanide," Claire said as she read the warrant.

"I don't even know what that is," Sam stated as a matter of fact.

"It's a poison that makes it appear someone died of a heart attack. But in this case, the preliminary report had stated stabbed to death. Apparently the final report came out today, and Detective Jones hurried over here to try and find the poison."

Greg turned cold eyes onto Detective Barnett as he said, "Jones decided Sam was guilty from the get-go. I've worked enough crime scenes and with enough detectives to know when someone sets his mind and then tries to find the evidence to match his decision."

Detective Barnett looked like it was all he could do not to speak up. Would it be for his partner, or would it be to agree with Greg? Sam wondered. In her heart, she felt this detective was trying to follow evidence. He didn't seem to be on the same page as Detective Jones.

Thank You, Lord.

All of a sudden the voices moved into the kitchen. It sounded like they were tearing the place apart. Making balls with her fists, it was all she could do to sit, be quiet, and stay calm. It would all work out in the end. She knew she was innocent. God would prove her innocence. She would be a testimony to Him, and He would be a testimony of her innocence.

Scanning the various faces, Sam realized they were all talking, all but the detective, but she had missed the majority of the conversation. It was probably for the best. If she listened, she might find herself becoming anxious and Sam didn't want to go there. For the next ten minutes, she sat back against the couch, closed her eyes, and whispered prayers to the Lord. He was the only one who could save her, and while He did what she couldn't do, she wanted to wait in peace. His peace.

When the back screen door slammed, Sam jumped.

The detective stepped over to the swinging door and glanced into the kitchen. Returning to his original place, he leaned against the wall again. "They're moving the search outside, ma'am. It looks like we're almost through. Sorry for the inconvenience." Detective Barnett gave a slight nod.

"Can we move to the kitchen? I'll fix us some cool glasses of lemonade," Sam said. "How does that sound?"

"Like a great idea," Claire said as she followed Sam's lead to the kitchen.

"Let me make it, Sam." Margaret said as she hurried around the line walking into the kitchen. The detective was the last one in line.

Everyone fell silent as they stopped in their tracks. Margaret let out a squeak as she covered her mouth with both hands. Dropping them slowly, she said, "Oh my gosh!"

Sam looked around the room. "What have they done?"

Things had been pulled out of every cabinet. Stuff was strewn on the floor and stacked on the counters. It was a mess.

Picking the gallon pitcher up off the countertop, Sam blew out a breath of agitation. "I was going to say, let me do it. I need to stay busy, but it looks like there is enough work here to keep us both busy for a while. So for now, Margaret, help me make the lemonade. Grab two cans out of the freezer. Everyone sit. Ignore the mess. I am." She forced her focus on finding the big spoon to mix the lemonade.

Everyone sat, except the detective. He remained standing with his back to the swinging door. His face showed almost as much displeasure as Samantha felt, but she wasn't going to give in to it. That would make Jones too happy when he came back inside with nothing to charge her for. At least he would have the satisfaction of knowing he ruined her home. She could only imagine what the rest of the house looked like. For the time being, she wasn't going to think about it, because she was not going to give him the satisfaction.

Cover me in peace, Lord, and let it be real.

In no time, the lemonade was mixed and ice filled five glasses. Sam poured them as Margaret passed them out. When it came to the last two glasses, Sam grabbed them both. She extended one toward the detective.

"I really don't need it. Thanks."

"Please? For me. Just take it. I didn't poison it," she said with a smile. "I promise."

The detective returned her smile as a slight chuckle slipped past his lips, making Sam's smile deepen. She knew he believed in her innocence. He took the lemonade she offered.

Holding her glass, she joined the three at the table. After taking her first sip, she sighed. "I hope they finish soon. Marty will be out of school shortly. I don't want him coming home to them or this mess."

"Don't worry. I'll help you and Margaret. We'll have everything shipshape before he gets home," Greg said.

"It shouldn't be much longer, ma'am. How many storerooms do you have outside?" the detective questioned.

Looking at the detective, she thought for a brief second. "Only two. One attached to the carport, my laundry room, and the other back in the corner of the lot."

"That's the one I stored the poison in," Margaret added.

The detective smiled at her.

"This lemonade sure hits the spot, Ms. Cain." Claire set her glass down on the table after swallowing another sip. "This is just part of the investigation, you know. It will be over soon. Eventually the police will get on the right trail and leave you alone. I'm sure. But if not, still don't worry. You're innocent. It will work out."

Claire sounded very sure of herself today. The other day at her office she sounded like she would do her best. But today, the woman sounded more confident. Apparently she'd done a little of her own investigating — or she'd been listening to Greg singing Samantha's praise. Either way, Sam was glad to hear her sound so confident.

The back door slammed again and every head turned in the direction of the sound. "I need your keys, Ms. Cain. Now."

Standing, Sam moved to the counter and picked them up. Pulling out the key to the ignition, making it stand separate from the rest, she handed the lot of them to the detective. "My car is the Camry under the carport." Sam smiled knowingly at the man. They hadn't found anything. That was why they were still looking, and it was killing him. His grim expression told her everything she needed to know.

Yes! She smiled.

He turned and walked back outside without saying a word.

Greg and Margaret both laughed as Sam strutted back over to the table and returned to her seat.

"That man is ridiculous," Margaret said. "He looks upset that he hasn't found anything to throw you in jail for. What is his problem?"

"I wish I knew," the detective said in a very low whisper. Not low enough, though.

"You and me both, sir," Sam said to the detective and his eyes opened wide as if he didn't realize he had spoken his thoughts aloud. She liked that. Proved even further, he was a man out for the truth, not ready to hang her just because his partner wanted to.

Detective Barnett focused swiftly on the floor, keeping his gaze away from the people at the table. He was probably berating himself for speaking his thoughts aloud. Sam almost felt sorry for him, but he didn't need to worry. His partner didn't hear anything and he, for sure, wouldn't hear it from any of them.

The next few minutes were spent in silence. No one had anything to say, but it was all right. Everyone knew what was going through each other's mind. Sam just wished it would all be over soon.

The screeching of the back door pierced Sam's ears as Detective Jones yanked it open and stepped inside. He dropped the keys on the counter, looked at his partner, and gave a nod. "We're going now." Turning his sour face toward Samantha, he said, "Ms. Cain, it's not over yet. I hope you understand we don't take murder lightly."

She rose from her seat and moved closer to the overconfident man who was speaking. "I hope you understand, Detective, I too do not take murder lightly. Nor do I take the invasion of my home lightly. I've done nothing wrong and the sooner you figure that out and get your mind in the investigation, the sooner you'll find the true killer, because it isn't me." On that, she turned her back on him, looked at the other detective, and gave him a short nod. Hopefully he understood her silent words. She couldn't afford to lose someone who was on her side.

"Detective Jones, before you go," Claire

said as she rose to her feet, "I need you to e-mail or fax me a copy of the final ME report. By the warrant, I see the ME changed his preliminary findings." She pulled her business card out of the side pocket on her purse and extended the card toward the detective.

His brown eyes darkened, and he snatched it from her hand. "I'll send it to you when I return to the station." The two left out the back door as the screen door slammed behind them.

Margaret moved over to shut the wooden door, not making a sound. Quietly, she turned back toward everyone and said softly, "It's over. Right?"

"For now, Margaret." Greg moved next to her, rubbing her forearms gently as if trying to reassure her, and then draped one arm over her shoulder, pulling her next to his side.

Sam grimaced. "Unfortunately that man believes I'm guilty, and he's going to keep digging, trying to find something to make the courts agree to arrest me. But he won't succeed. My God is bigger than he is."

"That's right," Margaret said, smiling sweetly.

As bad as it seemed, Sam knew she could only take one day at a time and wait on the

Lord to direct her and Greg in their next step to clear her name. She smiled, filled with hope for her future. "Claire, thanks for coming on such short notice," she said as she led her to the front door.

"I'm only a phone call away. Don't panic, and don't let that bully torment you." She patted Sam's shoulder as she headed out the front door.

Closing the door behind her, Sam turned back to her friends, whom she considered like family, and said, "Let's get busy. We have less than fifteen minutes to turn this place around before Marty gets home."

CHAPTER 18

Mark listened to Ben Jones' grumbling all the way back to the station. The young detective couldn't wait to get out of that enclosed space. So many times he wanted to open his mouth to his senior partner and try to correct his statements, but deep inside, he knew he'd be wasting his breath. Ben Jones didn't want to look at the truth. He had it in his mind to condemn this woman, and Mark had no idea why.

Although he had tried several times to get Jones to admit his accusing notions about Samantha Cain were ludicrous, the detective would not agree. He stood by his convictions that he was following the evidence. Mark knew better but couldn't turn that hardheaded man's thoughts around, so he accepted defeat quietly. He planned to continue his pursuit in finding the true evidence that would point toward the real killer.

Standing on the sidelines as Samantha Cain, the retired detective, and the woman they called Margaret talked among themselves, Mark couldn't help but notice the belief they had in Ms. Cain's innocence. He thought so, too. His gut told him that he and his partner were chasing the wrong scent, but he couldn't get Ben to believe him, believe his instincts. Mark needed to learn more about the victim. Whom did the man cross enough to be killed? Besides, usually you looked to the spouse, and Ben hadn't even given that woman a first glance, let alone a second.

If we don't investigate the man, we'll never find the truth, and that is our job.

So Mark was going to do just that. Ben could follow his take on the evidence found so far, even the planted evidence in Mark's opinion. He felt certain there was more evidence to be found, and, given a little more time, he'd find the right trail to follow to find the guilty party.

Besides, he didn't read the crime scene evidence in the same light that his partner had read it. Although the crime scene had blood spatter and blood pooled around the wound and on the floor, it didn't show major blood spatter as you'd normally find in a stabbing. And, besides, how could that little woman get close enough to take such a big man down with one swing of the letter opener?

Luck? I don't think so.

The poison in the blood could help explain things a little better. Maybe she gave him poison in a cup of coffee, and then, while he was close to passing out, she stabbed him and left him there to bleed out. But in the back of Mark's mind, he still felt the crime scene lacked signs of a struggle. No furniture was overturned. His desk was neatly organized. Nothing was out of place. Not even one of his many pictures was knocked over. As far as the blood spatter was concerned, one jab wouldn't spray much, but something still boggled his mind. How would she know the one exact spot to jab with the letter opener? No.

Was she aiming for the heart? Or for the lung? Both would kill him. Puncturing the lung would be a slow death, as well as bleeding out, unless, of course, she sliced his throat, cutting the carotid artery. He would have bled out with every pump of his heart. Now that would have sprayed and pooled some blood.

With his lung punctured, oxygen would have to be cut off from the brain for about five minutes for him to die. It was an odd way to asphyxiate the man, but it would work. What Mark needed to do was read in full the final report on the cause of death. Was the COD poison? Loss of blood? Or loss of oxygen? Someone truly wanted this man to die, and it looked like they wanted Samantha Cain to take the rap for it. That to Mark was obvious. Why couldn't Ben see it, too?

Inside the station, Mark watched Jones walk straight to his desk and, from that moment on, he didn't open his mouth again. That suited Mark just fine. Instead, Jones plopped himself in his chair and logged onto his computer.

Now that was a strange sight . . . a man who didn't like the computer going straight to it.

Mark couldn't help but wonder what the man was up to. Surely, he wasn't going to dig for more information on the victim or look for other clues surrounding his death. Things he should be doing. No, not Ben Jones.

Mark smirked as he fought to hold back the laughter that wanted to bubble up from within. Then he turned his thoughts, as well as his computer, on to the things he was checking earlier. Glancing back over the things he had copied and pasted from Ken

Richardson's chatter from his different media sites, Mark was more convinced than ever that some of these chats meant more than what they seemed to mean on the surface.

As quick as his computer dinged, telling him he had a new message, Mark checked his e-mails to see if his favorite geek from IT had responded yet.

Seven new messages. Yes. And one was from Kevin. The real names would be a great help; if the geek wonder could have gotten those, it would make Mark's life easier, or at least his investigation. Kevin was a smart dude. He knew how to get around walls, find hidden passwords and messages and get into places most ordinary users didn't even know existed. If there were any hidden messages or secret codes, he would find them.

Clicking on the message, it appeared, and Mark started reading.

All right.

Instantly he saw that Kevin, too, thought it was coded messages. The "boy wonder" couldn't break the code, not yet anyway, but he felt certain the conversations dealt with a product being available and setups to meet at various times and places for selling or buying the product. Kevin managed to find IP addresses on most of the chatters. Some of the addresses piggybacked so many times going to so many places all over the world that it made it difficult to find the origin. For those, Kevin was not able to find all the owners . . . yet. But Mark wouldn't lose faith in his Computer Genius. Most of the people Richardson communicated with on his media sites, thank God, weren't smart enough to hide like the ones who hopped around the world.

By attachment, Kevin sent him a list of names and addresses he had gathered so far.

Pulling them up, Mark printed the list off. After retrieving the paper, he started checking for rap sheets on any of them. Two had records. One was arrested several times on petty misdemeanors while another one was arrested for distributing drugs.

Oh, this is good. Maybe the victim was selling drugs. Mr. Innocent, I knew he wasn't. Now I just need to find proof of whatever he was doing.

The two people with priors was where he would start his investigation, but not with Detective Jones. He had to do this on his own. When he found something concrete, something that could open Jones' mind to other possibilities, then he would start sharing. It was for the best. Normally Jones was a good cop, but for some reason he wasn't on spot with this investigation. Mark really needed to find out what was messing with the detective's mind. If he could find that out, maybe he could help his partner look beyond his nose. He quickly jotted down the addresses of the two parties of interest, as well as their job sites and their parole officers. This was a great start.

He glanced across the desks. Jones was still messing with his computer. Must be playing games.

Mark sighed. This case was going to take them a long time to solve at the rate they were going. The first forty-eight hours, when the trail was really hot, was usually the best time to solve a case, but this wasn't going to be one of them.

With confidence, Mark looked back through his copy of the paper file. He didn't have a copy of the completed autopsy in his file yet. Glancing back at the other six messages, he found a message from the ME he was copied on. Quickly he pulled it up. It was the latest report on the Richardson murder. After hitting the print button, he scanned the report, already knowing the final COD was poison.

Why stab him? Hurrying up the death? What

was the point? In his gut he felt this, too, was more of a setup to make Samantha Cain look like the guilty party. When the machine quit making a whirling sound and the paper shot out, he grabbed the hard copy and added it to his folder. Glancing through the rest of the pages, including notes from the interviews, he felt a gnawing in his gut, but what?

Something kept tugging at the back of his mind. He knew there was something that wasn't right but couldn't bring it to the front. Clasping his fingers, he turned them down and out, cracking his knuckles. His thoughts kept flipping the pages in his mind.

Finally he sighed and shook his head.

He'd start with the leads he had just found and hopefully that nagging feeling would surface soon with the answer on what was missing or bothering him, or at least with the right question to ask.

Mark needed to get a warrant so he could pull the info from the telephone company. He needed the erased messages on Richardson's texting as well as any deleted phone calls. Mark turned a few more pages over and found the victim's cell phone information.

He dashed off an e-mail to Patricia Reynolds, ADA, a friend of his in the

District Attorney's office, and gave her the case file number, victim's name and address, and the home phone and cell numbers. He asked to get a warrant to get copies of incoming and outgoing calls from the home number, as well as erased numbers and texts from the cell phone. He made sure he covered all aspects of what he needed. Mark didn't want anything to backfire down the road, keeping him from being able to use what he would find.

In the e-mail, he explained that it was only him asking because his partner already believed he'd found the guilty party and wouldn't look any further. He gave her what he had so far to back up his reason for pursuing this line of investigating so she could get the warrant, and Mark explained to Patricia how he really believed they were going down the wrong trail and needed her help desperately, but to keep it on the QT.

After sending his request off, he didn't worry in the least about Patricia ignoring his request. She knew how Jones worked. The man believed in old school still being the best way — letting gut override evidence. Sure, they did great things in the old days and took down many a criminal, but also some innocent people went to prison when a cop tried to go purely by his gut instinct.

About the time Mark's computer dinged and a box popped up, saying "new message," Jones rose. "I'm going for lunch. Are you ready to eat?"

Mark glanced at his partner and then back at the box on his screen. It had to be Patricia. Scrunching his face, he said, "I'm not really hungry. I have something to take care of, so if it's okay with you, I'll do it while you go do your lunch. How does that sound?" Mark figured he could swing by Mickey D's and that would do him just fine. Eat on the run; he did it all the time.

"You kids today. You never eat. No wonder you stay so skinny." Grabbing his rumpled jacket off the back of his chair, Jones said, "Take your time. Nothing's really going on today. I've got to figure out our next move. We've got to find the poison and link it to Cain, or something more concrete to get that woman. To connect her to the crime."

Sitting back in his chair, Mark said, "Jones, let me in on your secret. Why are you so dead sure she did it?"

The man's eyes darkened. Pinning his gaze on Mark, he said, "You know who she is, don't you? I know you weren't here when her husband was killed, but go do a little detective work. You'll see why I believe she's guilty. People don't change." Turning his back on his partner, Jones headed toward the exit as he stuffed his arms into his jacket sleeves and tugged it on.

Yeah, Mark knew who she was. She was the woman engaged to a fellow police officer. A great cop. There was no way Matthew Jefferies would fall in love with a cop killer, had she truly killed her husband — and Mark knew that was what Jones was insinuating. He'd look it up, but he doubted what Ben Jones was thinking was reality.

"Enjoy your lunch. I'll see you later," Mark said as his partner was stepping out the door. He had other things to do at the moment.

Scanning the e-mail from Patricia, he found she had his warrant.

That was quick.

Reading further, he noticed she was not on this case so the QT worked both ways. The warrant would be on legal record showing the policeman who requested it and the attorney who got it, but that was not important. The important thing was not to talk about it, drawing attention to what they had done. If it ever came out, it would be after it helped catch the true culprit and then no one would care who requested the warrant. In fact, Mark was pretty sure Ben would gladly take the credit.

Great. She got it. That was all that mattered.

Mark had no plans of telling anyone who helped him get the warrant. As his hopes heightened and a smile touched his lips, Mark decided he would slip by her office and pick it up. Afterward he would grab a bite to eat. He could chow down on his Mickey D's on the way to the telephone company.

His heart pounded as he rose. Mark knew he was finally starting to get somewhere on this case.

Grabbing his blazer and slipping it on, he hurried out the door.

Today he was going to get the lead that would take Jones' fixation off of Samantha Cain and turn this case around.

CHAPTER 19

All three hustled around the house, setting everything in its place. Greg took Marty's room, since most were toys to throw back in his toy box, clothes to realign in the closet, shoes to set straight, and refold some of the clothes in the drawers . . . an easy job compared to the rest, and then he ran out back to check the storage room, making sure it was locked up again.

Meanwhile, Margaret and Sam tackled the kitchen together, and then each ran off to straighten their own bedrooms. The bathrooms followed that and were another easy fix, refolding and stacking towels back on the shelf, followed with straightening and organizing the medicines in the cabinet.

When finished, all three collapsed in the living room.

Moments later, Marty scurried through the front door. "Hey, hey, hey," he shouted as he raced across the living room toward the kitchen. "What's my snack for today?" The whole time he was wiggling out of his backpack, getting ready to toss it down at his convenience.

Sam smiled to herself.

Margaret held up her hand to Samantha. "I got this. You rest. I'm sure the two of you need to talk." As she spoke she looked from Samantha to Greg.

The room grew quiet as Sam's thoughts tumbled out. "Greg, what about the terminal manager who was let go just before they replaced him with Ken? Or even our chief dispatcher, who was passed —"

The phone rang, cutting off her words.

"Passed over for terminal manager when they hired Ken." She reached out to grab the phone. "Hello."

"Sam. Hey, it's me, Pat."

Her stomach dropped as she heard the voice of the dispatcher who relieved her every morning. She stood quickly, holding the phone so tightly her hand hurt. What was he calling for? As concerned as she was, she tried not to let it sound in her voice. "Hi, Pat. What's up? Someone got sick and they need me to fill in?"

"No. I wish." He sighed.

His tone twisted a knot into her stomach. She saw in her mind's eye Pat stroking his dark beard as he tried to form his words. What was going on? She held onto the receiver with both hands, attempting to stay steady.

Apparently Greg saw the movement because he jumped to his feet and stepped to her side.

"Oh no, Pat. Something is wrong. I hear it in your voice. What happened?"

Greg stood silently next to her.

"I'm sorry to be the one to tell you, but you know how it works. All the bad news to share they dump on us in the dispatch office. You'd think the chief dispatcher would be calling you, but no. He passed it on to me." He chuckled. "And we always thought it was just Ken who did that. This comes down from the main office. They have suspended you, without pay, while you're under investigation for Ken Richardson's death."

"What?" She drew in a short breath. "That's not fair." Her knees wobbled.

Quickly, Greg caught her by the elbow and gently helped her sit down.

"But, Pat, I didn't do it. I wouldn't. You know that."

"We all know that, honey. No one here thinks you're guilty. In fact, all the drivers and mechanics keep asking about you —

how you're doing through all of this. None of us have called, 'cause while you're off, we're hoping you're getting a break from all of this commotion at work dealing with his death."

"Oh, Pat. Will this ever end? Please tell everyone I miss them and I wish I was there. Also tell them to keep me in their prayers and stand strong on believing my innocence."

"Honey, you know we will. Everyone around here loves you. Take care. And if we can do anything, don't hesitate to ask." Encouragement poured out of Pat's voice.

"Thanks so much. You don't know how much that means to me." On those words they said their good-byes.

"More bad news?" Greg asked.

After she shared with Greg that her job had given her an unlimited time of personal leave, Margaret walked in and caught the tail end. But she heard enough to cause a reaction. "They did what? That's not fair! How could they? You, who stand true to your friends, your boss, and your company, even when faithfulness is not deserved. Your company should be standing behind you." She gritted her teeth, seething with anger.

"It's probably for the best, Margaret. When I'm at work, everyone wants to talk about it, and I'm wishing I was home trying to help clear my name." Reality clicked, and she looked at Greg. "Well, now I can."

Greg smiled slightly. "Everything always works out for the best."

"Now I can do what I was in the middle of suggesting to you when the phone rang. What do you think about us going to see TJ Perry together? I know where he works. Maybe he knows something that could help us. Or maybe he knows someone who could give us some helpful information."

"That's not a bad idea, Sam. When the main office let him go and put this guy in his place, he probably did a little research on his own. I know I would."

Margaret laid her hand on Greg's shoulder. "I knew you two would figure out something. Don't you worry about Marty. I'll see he does his homework before playing. If y'all are a little late, I'll shoo him to take his bath. We'll be fine. And don't forget, steak and gravy. Dinner will be ready when you return."

When Greg's gray eyes flashed in Margaret's direction, her face flooded in a haze of red, but her smile showed her pleasure.

"I also thought we might try to catch Dean at home tomorrow. As Chief Dispatcher, he works Monday through

Friday and is off every weekend. Ken was the one who hired him. We didn't have a chief dispatcher before. Those two were pretty tight without obviously crossing the line in front of all of us at work. They never let on that they saw each other after hours, nor did they talk like they knew one another beforehand. Dean Smith does a good job, so I never thought foul play there, even though I thought the job should have gone to Pat. But Dean might know more and be able to shed some light on Ken's life. I think he likes my work, so he probably wouldn't have a problem talking to you in front of me."

"Let's have a cup of coffee and then hit the road," Greg suggested. "Clearing your calendar just opened up some doors, don't you think?" He lifted his brows up and down like Groucho Marx.

The women laughed, and Margaret hustled out, leading the three of them to the kitchen.

"The cookies were good, but how long before we get fresh baked again?" Marty said as they entered. He threw his napkin in the garbage, then placed his empty glass in the sink.

"Oh you," Sam said as she roughed up his hair. "Be thankful you have a snack. There are kids around the world who don't even get three meals a day."

"Aw, Mom, I wasn't complaining. I was just asking. Can't a kid ask a question without hearing about the problems around the world?"

They all laughed. The boy was such a little grown-up for only being in the third grade. What he said was sad but true, but with the problems they had in their own backyard, she couldn't help herself. She was probably trying too hard to find something else to keep the focus off the troubles at hand. Squatting in front of him, she hugged him tightly. "I love you, Marty. I hope you always know that."

"Gee. Women." Marty looked to Greg and rolled his eyes.

Greg almost doubled over in laughter. Between bellows, he said, "He's so young, but already he knows there is no understanding women." The laughter spread around the room.

Marty looked about, as if to say the whole roomful of adults had gone crazy. Shaking his head and shrugging, he asked, "Can I go play outside?"

"Homework first. And, sweetie, I'm going to be leaving with Uncle Greg for a little while, but Margaret is here for you. Be good and mind her." She winked at him as he nodded. "Thanks, buddy."

An hour later, Greg turned his car into the parking lot of Big Truck Services, a competitor of the company where Sam worked. When she called TJ, he told them to come on over, and he would talk to them.

TJ met them at the door garbed in a neatly pressed white cotton shirt, with the company's logo embroidered in dark blue thread across the pocket, and a pair of navy blue chinos. Sam remembered him well. He worked hard and always did a wonderful job. His country-boy smile and accent won the hearts and trust of many customers, as well as drivers over the years. "Hi, Samantha. Good to see you, honey. Sorry for all the trouble you're having." His bald head reflected the overhead fluorescent lights while his snow-white, neatly trimmed goatee made him look distinguished.

"I appreciate you taking time to see us, TJ. Greg, my friend here, is going to ask you a few questions that might help me clear my name," she said as she shook his extended hand. Truck drivers shared gossip like women; it was no wonder he already knew what she was going through.

After shaking Greg's hand, TJ said, "I

hope I can help. Follow me." While leading them down a hall and into what looked like a conference room, he said, "I can't believe anyone would think you'd kill that man — or anyone for that matter. Don't tell me you're not the same sweet Sam you've always been." He chuckled slightly. "I warned you before moving into the dispatch office that those drivers and that job would change you." He winked. "But into a killer, no less. I never thought it would change you that much." He grinned and shook his head.

She knew he was only picking at her and trying to make things a little more comfortable for all three. She smiled. "Yes, you did warn me. And don't you worry one little *pea-picken* bit. I'm still the same old me." Sam imitated his country twang and tossed her hair behind her shoulders one side at a time.

Both laughed heartily as Sam tilted her chin in the air. When the laughter settled, TJ motioned for them to take a seat. "Would either of you care for coffee?" Both declined. The man fixed himself a cup and then joined them at the table. "Now, what kind of questions can I help you with?"

Greg pulled a small tablet from his inside jacket pocket and snatched a pen from his shirt pocket. *That was probably how he did it in the old days,* Sam thought. He looked in-charge and ready for business.

"Can you give me any personal things, assumptions, known facts, anything overheard or told to you about Ken Richardson? Do you have any idea what the man was doing before Bulk hired him?"

"First, let me say, I did not know Ken Richardson at all. He wasn't a local Terminal Manager with any of our competitors, so I never met him at plants when the carriers called us together for their company meetings that meant we had to change something or they had changed something. The kind of meetings where they tried to play us against one another, but in a hushed way, to bring us down on our charges."

Greg nodded, letting him know he understood what he meant.

"Anyway, I heard he was fired from his last job. He was Terminal Manager for a trucking company in Mississippi for about three years. It burned my innards that they ran me off to replace me with someone who had lost his job. I wondered what was up. It was so convenient. They let me go at the same time he became available. Then reality hit and I remembered I was 'technically' fired, too." He made quotes with his fingers. "Well, I was given a choice to resign or be fired. I knew I didn't do anything wrong, so I chose the former. Maybe Ken was innocent, too, so I chose to give him the benefit of the doubt and just believe the company was ready for someone new."

"Our loss," Sam added softly.

"So you never did any research on the man?" Greg asked.

"No. But so many different Operational Managers of different plants Bulk was connected to let me know how much they missed working with me over there. But my loss was Big Truck Services gain. I'm not trying to pat myself on the back, but they got their foot in the door, so to speak, because they hired me and those guys at the plants I mentioned liked working with me. So a little here and a little there, BTS now services some of the same plants. Sure, we're a smaller company, but I kind of like that. So does my wife. I'm not nearly as stressed when I go home at night, and I go home at an earlier hour."

Sam smiled. "I'm sure Helen loves that."

Greg twisted his lips from one side to the other. "So it sounds like you don't have anything that would help me. I mean, help Sam."

TJ's lips disappeared as the edges turned up slightly. It was almost a haughty look, but in a helpful sort of way. Sam knew immediately he knew something but was hesitant about sharing.

"Tell us, TJ. Please. We never know what is going to help."

"I don't like to talk about people or spread rumors, but I can tell you something I've been told by more than one Operations Manager, so there must be a little truth to it."

"That's what we're looking for," Greg said. "We just need to show the police that Ken Richardson was no saint and other people might have had motive to kill him. Everyone has him pictured as a saint, and I believe that's why the police are looking so hard at Samantha instead of looking elsewhere. They need another lead to follow. Right now she's all they've got."

TJ glanced around before speaking, then lowered his voice. "According to a few of the plant managers who make the decisions as to which company gets the haul, he's made some under-the-table offers to them. A chance for them to receive kickbacks or some extra side benefits, if you know what I mean."

Greg and Samantha both looked at him and then at each other.

"Really?" Sam was shocked. This was big,

and she knew it. Hopefully there was still enough time to find something . . . a deal gone wrong maybe?

"Don't get me wrong. It hasn't been all of them who have told me such things, but it is more than a couple."

Greg's brows shifted slightly. "The ones who haven't said anything might be the ones who went in cahoots with Richardson's offer. You never know."

Silent looks were exchanged among the three at the table.

They talked for a little longer as Greg tried to get some names from TJ. Of course, he couldn't and wouldn't expose them. Some may have taken the offer for all he knew and he wasn't going to get any of them in trouble. They trusted him, and he couldn't afford to lose their trust. And that was why everyone liked TJ. A man of honor.

On the ride back to Sam's, Greg said, "Cheer up. It may help us. At the least it's a start, if I can get a little proof to back any of the rumors or gossip."

Sam leaned her head against the headrest. *Yes, but where do we start looking?* She shook her thoughts out of her head. It would be okay. It would all work out. "I'm not worried, Greg. I trust you. And more than that, I trust God. We'll get through this and the true culprit will be convicted. Not me."

She spoke boldly, but in her mind she whispered, *Lord, You know my true thoughts and even though I do trust You and Greg, my flesh is still a little shaky. Show us where to start. Please don't let this drag out too long. I'm not sure I can bear it — and I know Marty doesn't need the added tension, either.*

CHAPTER 20

The smell of steak smothered with onions and garlic, simmering on a low heat, led their steps straight into the kitchen. As they reached the table, Sam and Greg saw that their plates were filled and ready for consumption.

"I heard you drive up and the car doors slam. I hope you two don't mind, and I hope you're hungry."

"You'll hear no complaints from me, dear one." Greg kissed her cheek as he found his place at the table. "A man could get used to this, Margaret. You best beware." He cocked his head slightly.

She giggled, and Sam smiled. She was glad to hear a little joy spread through the room.

"Oh, Momma, did you hear that? I think Uncle Greg likes Ms. Margaret." In his elementary ways, Marty picked up on the romance in the air mingling with the smell of some good old home cooking.

"Marty," Margaret squealed as her face turned ten shades of red.

Everyone laughed. "I think the boy is reading my mind." Greg's smile deepened as he winked at Margaret.

After everyone calmed down, the blessing was said and all started filling their mouths with the delicious food.

Margaret cast a glance toward Marty and then settled her gaze on Samantha. "So, how did it go . . . if you don't mind me asking right now? It can wait, if you want."

"I think the meeting was productive. Although he didn't give us a lot, TJ gave us something to check into, a place to start. Don't you think?" Samantha directed her question to Greg.

Chewing the morsel already in his mouth, he finished it quickly so he could answer. "It went great. I think tomorrow we'll drop in on Dean, like you suggested. And tonight, when I get home, I'm going to make a few calls to some friends in high places, so to speak, and see if I can find out anything to back up what TJ shared with us. Sometimes Big Brother's watching and sees things we try to hide." He stirred the rice around in the gravy and said, "Pass the salt, please, little buddy."

Marty handed it to him.

Greg went on to say, "Big Brother is always watching. People think they are getting away with things, when in reality, most of those under-the-table deals are being noted. And sometimes they jump on them right away. Other times they wait until it's convenient to help Big Brother in something they are doing."

Sam's lips curled upward as hope started to rise a little higher.

The next day, Marty planted himself in front of the television set with cartoons spilling out and said, "Are you going to watch with me this morning, Momma? You look like you're dressed to go to work, but it's daytime."

Laughing, she said, "No work today. After we eat breakfast, Uncle Greg and I are going to run another errand together. Maybe tonight we can go see a movie, or rent a movie and pop some popcorn. What do you say to that?"

Jumping to his feet, he scurried over to his mother. Wrapping his arms around her waist, he said, "You are such a fun mommy. Thank you."

Holding him close and pressing her fingers against his curls, she leaned down and kissed the top of his head. "Of course I am. I have such a wonderful boy, what else could I be?"

He laughed and dropped his hands, then plopped back down in front of the TV. Within seconds he was lost in his make-believe world.

Thank You, Lord, for protecting him through all of this, she thought as she made her way to the kitchen. Coffee was already brewing and three empty cups sat fresh and clean on the counter waiting for their recipients. Margaret was standing by the stove, steadily cooking breakfast. Sam smelled the sizzling sausage and watched her slowly stirring the scrambled eggs as they cooked.

"Greg must be already on his way," Sam said as she noticed the table was set for four.

"If he doesn't want cold eggs, he better be pulling —" A knock on the back door interrupted Margaret's words. "Ah, great. He's here. Will you let him in please?"

Opening the door wide, Sam said, "You were about to miss out on hot eggs, but you made it just in time."

"I have a good feeling about today," Greg said as he walked into the kitchen. "I wouldn't dare mess it up by starting my day off wrong. Thanks for the invite, Margaret dear." He flashed her a wink.

"Greg called while you were in the shower. I told him if he hurried, he could be here in time to eat with us." Margaret opened the oven and pulled out a tray of piping hot, lightly tanned biscuits.

"I'll get Marty. It looks like breakfast is served." Sam stepped to the swinging door and held it open slightly. "Come on, Son. Breakfast is ready."

Sam didn't have to tell him twice. He jumped to his feet and dashed through the swinging door before it even came back on the first swing.

Greg had poured three cups of coffee and was carrying two to the table, so Sam grabbed the third one and joined them. She said grace and then they all dug into their food.

"I'm going to get fat if I keep hanging around here for all the meals," Greg said as he stuffed another bite of sausage and egg into his mouth.

"If?" Sam said as she picked up a buttered biscuit and spread a teaspoon of strawberry preserves in the middle. Out of the corner of her eye, she noticed Margaret silently watching Greg for his response. The poor woman seemed to be holding her breath as she tried not to appear to even notice anyone around the table.

"Okay, ladies. *When* I keep hanging around. I just didn't want to be so bold."

Sam giggled softly.

Quiet relief spread through Margaret's facial features. Sam had known her long enough to know that Greg could be bold, but Margaret wouldn't dare. "Greg, the door is always open to you. And it's kind of nice to have a man around, right, Margaret?" Sam said.

"What about me?" Marty cried out. "I thought I was your little man."

Everyone chuckled and Sam said, "Sorry, buddy. I wasn't thinking."

After the plates were empty, or close to it, Sam started clearing hers.

"You two go take care of business," Margaret said. "I've got this. It's the least I can do to help. Let me." She reached out for Sam's plate.

"Thanks." She handed over her plate and then turned her eyes on Greg. "Give me one minute, and I'll be ready."

"Take your time. I'm going to have one more cup of this delicious brew." He cast a smile to Margaret as he rose to help himself.

"Let me," she said softly as her lashes fluttered downward.

Sam slipped to the back to brush her teeth. At least for the time being everything

229

seemed to be as it should. Her heart felt light.

Within the half hour, she and Greg were driving to Dean's home. "You sure you didn't want me to call him first?"

"And give the man a chance to slip out or make up an excuse why he can't be bothered with you today? Not on your life."

Glancing his way, Sam said, "So what did you discover last night that gives you great expectations today?"

With no music on and the air down low, the steady hum of the tires rolling on the street sounded louder than normal. Sam wasn't sure if it was her nerves exaggerating things or what. Part of her thought Dean might be willing to be helpful, but in the back of her mind she had always believed he and the boss had a special connection and he might not be so willing to share.

"Turns out there's an ongoing investigation at one of our major gas plants right outside the city." Greg's words grabbed Sam's attention. "The plant manager contacted local authorities, and Ken Richardson's name is in the mix. That's really all I can tell you. Don't know if it has anything to do with his death. Maybe . . . maybe not." Greg swiftly glanced in Sam's direction, then just as quickly returned his gaze to the highway. "But I'm thinking your number one dispatcher who was hired directly by Ken Richardson himself might know more about Richardson's personal life and maybe something about this other situation — not that we can mention it, because it's an ongoing investigation. And, truthfully, we shouldn't know anything about it, not that I know much. In case he is involved in some way, we don't want to tip him off."

"You got that from your inside help? It sounds to me like you still have some pretty significant connections. That's great." She watched his maneuvering, turning one way and then the other. He knew exactly how to get to Dean Smith's home. Sam hadn't even thought about directions, even though she'd never heard of the subdivision. Dean wasn't one of the coworkers she cared to befriend, not that she would treat him poorly. That wasn't her way. "I just hope he has something to tell us that will help us find the police another lead."

"Don't worry, kiddo. If he doesn't, I still believe we'll find more on what TJ Perry told us. Your boss was in too deep with too many things not to have a few enemies. If that head homicide detective wasn't so bent on putting the blame on you, they might

231

have another lead on their own by now." Turning left into a subdivision, Greg slowed down his car. "Watch for 12469 Trailing Pines. This is his street coming up." He took a right, and they continued down the street.

"It'll be a couple blocks down on the left," Sam said as she eyed the first address on the right. It ended with an even number, 12202.

In minutes they were standing at the front door. Greg pressed the doorbell.

A woman in her midfifties with bright red hair, dressed in a tailored suit and light green pumps to match, opened the door and said, "May I help you?"

"We're here to see Dean. Is he around?" Greg did the talking.

She frowned as she turned toward the stairs. Hesitantly she said, "Yes he is, but . . . he's getting dressed. We need to be somewhere in the next hour."

"No problem," Greg said. "We'll only take a few minutes of his time, but it's important we talk to him today. May we come in?"

She backed up slowly. "Please do." Her manners took control as she directed them to the formal living room. "May I get you a cup of coffee?"

They refused the offer but both said thank you as they took the seat she indicated. If

Samantha wasn't mistaken, she felt certain the woman's lips turned up into a smile as they turned down the coffee. This emphasized to Sam that the woman was merely being polite but never meant the offer. Oh well. It didn't matter. Sam didn't want to be there any more than the woman wanted them there. She hoped the discussion they had with her husband would be fruitful but also quick. Dean was still a man she had no desire to know on a personal level. Something about him had kept her at arm's length from the beginning.

As footsteps descended the stairs, the redheaded woman called out, "Dean, you have company. They're waiting in the living room. He'll be right with you," she said as she made her exit. They passed shoulder to shoulder at the arched entryway, eyes locking for a mere breath.

Dean's bright blue eyes turned on Greg and then shifted to Sam. "Samantha," he exclaimed, almost with excitement, "what on earth are you doing here? And how are you? I hate what I'm hearing at work."

His face seemed sincere.

Greg and Sam rose. Greg reached out to shake the man's hand while Sam made quick introductions. "We're sorry to bother you at home, Dean, but I'm hoping you can help shed some light on some things."

"Sit. Sit. Please, by all means. Ask away." He pointed to the settee and then sat in the chair that was positioned at a 90-degree angle from the couch. "Anything I can do to help."

He sounds friendly enough. I just hope it's real. "Greg, you go ahead and ask the questions." Sam wanted him to take the lead, because she truly didn't know what to ask. The only thing she could think of was, "What do you know about our boss that would have gotten him killed?" That was a little too obvious. She figured Greg had a better way of approaching this.

"As you know, the police have focused all their energies on proving Samantha to be the guilty party."

Shaking his head, he agreed. "That's absurd." His words were directed at Greg, but his eyes rested on Sam. "The woman gives over 100 percent of her life to the company and has a life of her own. When would she find time to be a killer, too? You know it takes a special trait, and not a good one, in a person to actually kill someone else?"

Greg sat a little straighter at that remark. "I agree Sam isn't capable of killing anyone, but it's a well-proven fact anyone pushed hard enough can become a killer. But this wasn't the case with your boss. I'm hoping, you being the —"

Cutting his own words off, he looked to Sam for help on the wording, and she instinctively knew what he was looking for. "Chief dispatcher," she inserted.

"Yes. You, being the chief dispatcher, would have a little closer relationship with the boss. We're hoping you knew of someone who might have a little more reason to kill him."

His eyes opened wide. "I assure you, I know nothing of the kind."

"Mr. Smith, surely you know of his goings-on with some plant managers. Don't get me wrong. I didn't get any of this from Samantha, because she had no idea. But I have my sources and have connected with enough of them to know Ken Richardson was making money other than through his normal paycheck."

"But, but —"

Greg held his hand up as if in reassurance. "I'm not here blaming you or saying you are involved in any way. But he was your boss, and you were in on all the big deals. You know more about his business ways than anyone, as well as you know a little about his personal life, too. Right?"

Shaking his head, Dean rose to his feet. "No. Emphatically no. I assure you I don't know anything about Ken's goings-on outside of work. And as far as any business dealings that were unethical, if he did those, trust me to say, I knew nothing."

"Dean," Sam assured him as she snatched his hand, "we really aren't accusing you of anything. We were hoping Ken confided some things with you, to you." She tightened her hold on his hand.

He grabbed hold with his other hand and held on as if his life depended on it. "The only reason that man hired me instead of promoting within was to stir up agitation. He lived to aggravate. Ken wanted everyone to not trust anyone. Sam, I promise. I know nothing. I knew he was a cruel, evil man, but the pay was good, is good. I need the money, so I work hard and keep my nose clean."

She squeezed one more time and then dropped her hand. "I understand, Dean. We were hoping," Sam said, her voice revealing her disappointment. Suddenly she heard a noise coming near — a steady slapping followed by a thump. Turning toward the sound, Sam saw a cute little girl with red ponytails wobbling into the living room, propped up on her crutches.

"Hey, Daddy. Are we still going to the show?"

Greg and Sam stood as the little girl talked to her father.

"Yes, Princess. Daddy has company, but they are about to leave. Amanda, this is Samantha Cain. Daddy works with her. And this is her friend, Greg." Turning his eyes on Greg, he added, "Sorry. I didn't catch your last name."

"No problem. Greg Singleton, ma'am. Nice to make your acquaintance." Greg dropped to one knee in front of the little girl as he spoke. He bowed his head as if she were royalty.

"Tee-hee-hee. He's funny, Daddy." Turning her cheerful face back on the company, she said, "It's nice to meet you two, too." Then she giggled again.

Greg rose. "You have a nice time at the movies, Ms. Amanda. We won't keep your daddy any longer." Turning away from the little girl, he thanked Dean for his time. Sam added her thanks, and the two headed toward the front door.

Following them, Dean stopped them as they exited his home. "I can tell you, Ken was into a lot of things. Nothing I have proof of, but conversations I've overheard tell me the man had his hands in many pots, if you know what I mean."

Greg nodded.

Sam reached out and hugged Dean . . . something she'd never done before, but she felt led to do. She whispered, "Thanks so much, Dean. I'm sorry I listened to rumors. I've had the wrong idea about you all along. Take care. And God bless you." Sam fought to hold back the tears. The man had a lot on his plate, and unfortunately rumors made him out to be sinister and out to get each employee. Sam was glad to learn different today.

On the drive home no talking was done. Sam's eyes had been opened to a new way of perceiving the chief dispatcher. Talk had always made the boss and the chief dispatcher out to be best of friends. Well, she already knew rumors were just that. Rumors. She was glad to know the truth and prayed God would pour out his blessings on the Smith family.

When Greg turned into Sam's driveway, he said, "I'm not going to be coming in this time. I have a few things I need to check on."

Opening the door, Sam climbed out. "Margaret will be very disappointed that you won't be coming in. Can you come back in time for supper?"

He shrugged. "I'm not sure, kiddo. I'll call if I can make it. Plan on not seeing me until tomorrow. Y'all are going to church, I presume?"

"Yes. We'll be there."

"I'll see you three then. Save me a seat."

On that, Greg put his car in reverse and backed out of the drive. He must really have a hot lead. Sam couldn't figure out what that could possibly be. If anything, they hit a dead end today. As she headed to the front porch, she heard in her spirit, *"I will never leave you nor forsake you. Trust in Me and stay in peace."*

That was the best advice she'd heard in a long time and she felt her spirits lift as she opened the front door. She would cast her cares on the Lord. Worry about nothing and pray about everything with thanksgiving. That was what the Word told her to do, and it had been her motto or direction every day for most of her life. No time to stop now.

"Marty, Margaret, I'm home," she called as she stepped into the living room.

CHAPTER 21

Mark Barnett stuffed a couple of hot fries in his mouth as he pulled out onto the street. With every bite of his Big Mac and sip of his Coke, he drew closer to the telephone company. The stirring of excitement stimulated him with each passing mile. The answer, the truth, was around the corner, and he would find it.

A short time ago, Mark had shoved the warrant in his top jacket pocket. "I appreciate the help. This should assist us in connecting to the real killer. In my gut, I believe this was a well-thought-out murder. Definitely premeditated. So well planned, the killer even set it up for someone else to take the fall. Finding Samantha Cain guilty is just too easy, if you know what I mean."

Nodding she said, "You already convinced me, Mark; now convince Ben." Patricia smiled as she walked him to the door. "I'm here if you need anything else. And please keep me posted how it goes."

Riding down the elevator, he laid his hand on his jacket's lapel. Folded neatly below it was all the help he needed at the moment. Anticipation started growing.

In no time he pulled into Richardson's phone carrier's parking lot. Inside the building he found the manager. After flashing his badge and his winning smile, he introduced himself. With fingers pinching the warrant, he knew the power this little slip of paper held. With confidence, he handed the warrant to the petite woman. After glancing it over, the manager led the way to the back of the store, where she stepped into an office. Apparently the woman decided they needed privacy for this transaction.

It worked for Mark. Whatever it took to get the info he needed.

"Now, Detective Barnett, what can I do for you? What exactly is this?"

"That's a warrant for Ken Richardson's cell and home phone activity. This also includes the text messages to and from that number," he said as he pointed.

Holding the paper in her hands, Mark could see her eyes moving as she rescanned the document. Her brows flickered occasionally as she read. A few minutes of silence filled the office. Finally she lowered the paper and locked her gaze on him. She nodded ever so slightly as she appeared to be thinking things through.

Finally a smile touched her lips. "I want to help you, but I have to get approval from the main office first. Give me a minute, and we'll see what they say."

"You don't really need their approval. That warrant gives you all the permission you need."

She tucked her head slightly, batted her lashes, and flashed a seductive smile his way. "Detective, you wouldn't want to see me lose my job now, would you?" She reached her polished nails out and laid her hand gently on his arm and gave it a squeeze. "It's procedure. We have to."

He sighed. "Go right ahead." He glanced at her nametag as he added, "Miss Lynette. I wouldn't want you to lose your job."

"Have a seat, please." Lynette motioned toward the chair sitting to the side of her desk and then sat down behind it. She made the call to her supervisor and then faxed the main office a copy of the warrant. Afterward she flipped her long blond curls behind her shoulders, flashed him another smile, and then proceeded to key in the information she needed for the warrant. When she finished, she dipped her shoulders one at a time and then said, "You see. I'm here to serve. Oh wait." She chuckled as she tossed her head back slightly, then pointed one of her manicured fingers in his direction. "That's your job." Her smile deepened as she searched his face, waiting for him to get her little joke.

Mark nodded. "Right. My job is to serve and protect. Cute." *Just get me what I need, woman.* He wanted to roll his eyes and show his irritation but instead kept his gleaming smile pasted in place.

A whirling sound from her printer started up and papers started filling the holder. In less than a minute it stopped. She tapped a few more keys and the noise of the machine started up again. When the noise quieted again, she grabbed the pages from the printer, separated them in two stacks, stapled each stack, and then handed them to Mark. "There you go, sir. All nice and neat." She rose and walked around to the side of the desk. Leaning slightly against it, she laid her manicured hand atop of her chest and said in a breathy voice, "If I can do anything else to help you, just let me know." Her smile said more than her words dared to say.

Mark stood. He thanked her for her time and walked out. With his looks, flirting women were at every turn. But his mind was strictly on business.

By the time he returned to the office, he found Ben back at his desk, sitting in his chair skimming through his computer.

"Something up?" Mark asked, hoping the answer would be no.

Ben shook his head, never looking up. "Things are kind of dead at the moment. I'm doing a little background check on our Little Miss Innocent."

The sarcasm in his voice made Mark want to laugh, but the only thing funny was Ben doing research on the computer. Nothing about Ms. Cain and her innocence was funny. Mark believed it was fact even though the circumstantial evidence said otherwise. If only Ben would do research on Ken Richardson instead. Shaking his head, he knew it wasn't worth the breath it took to tell him so.

"Did you look up her history with Officer Cain like I'd suggested you do? It wouldn't hurt to get you on the same page I'm on. In fact, it would make things a heck of a lot easier." The old man leaned back in his chair. "We'd probably have her behind bars right now if you'd do your little magic on the computer. I bet you could find all the backstory that could bring this case together so we could hand it over to the DA."

Mark shook his head slightly, wanting to tell his partner he was insane. Instead, he took a deep breath, then said, "I'm checking into things. I want to close this case as much as you. And then move on to the next. You know I don't like murders to drag out. The longer we take solving it, the harder it becomes to solve."

Ben's gaze darted from Mark's face to the paperwork he was pulling from his breast pocket. "Whatcha got?"

Not ready to share yet, Mark said, "Nothing yet. But I'm looking for connections like you said. Something that will bring it all together." Mark laid those pages on his desk, sat down in his chair, and flipped on his computer.

"That's my boy." A grin spread on the old man's face as he turned back to his own computer.

Let him think what he wanted. At least that would keep him off Mark's back for the time being.

Grabbing the folder tucked away neatly in his locked drawer, he set it next to him and then started reading Ken Richardson's texts — those he sent and those he received. Mark didn't go back the whole year as the warrant called for. He only went back one month. He figured if nothing jumped out at him in the last month of the man's life, then he would go back another month.

The next thirty minutes he spent perusing page after page, focusing on one contact person at a time, reading the texts back and forth for the entire month. It turned out he texted thirty individuals on a regular basis, five being family members. Nothing too interesting on the home front, but there were ten different people where the conversations sounded questionable — with some possibly buying and others possibly selling. One even sounded like a possible love interest.

Now that's something we haven't thought of, or should I say, something we haven't looked into. So far everyone has painted him as the perfect family man. Normally the wife is the first one we look at. I'll go back to that angle later.

Trafficking drugs usually gave motive for a lot of killings. Mark felt certain that was the lead to follow now. A more powerful motive. Money was almost always a big factor in murder.

It looked like he had another job for Kevin, the IT expert. Making two copies of the last month of texts, he slid one into his file folder and the other he slipped into a manila envelope. Slipping his file folder and the original copy of the year of texts and calls on Richardson's cell, as well as the copy of the home phone calls, incoming and outgoing, inside his middle desk drawer, he glanced around. No one seemed to be watching, especially Ben, and while the coast was clear, he quickly locked the drawer shut.

Sliding the keys back into his pocket, he rose. "I'm running upstairs. Be back shortly. If something comes up and we need to hit the road, beep me."

Ben grunted in agreement but never took his gaze off of his computer screen.

Mark took the steps two at a time. It was quicker than waiting on the slow elevator. Opening the door, he stepped out into the hallway and turned right, heading for Kevin's office. The hall was quiet, but he knew when he walked through IT's door, he would hear the humming and buzzing of all the computers that kept everything up and running throughout the department.

He stepped in and closed the door behind him. *Just as I thought.* How people worked with the steady whirring all day long, he would never know. It was enough hearing the energetic activity from the copiers and desktop computers they had running in homicide's room.

His shrewd friend's face was buried in his computer screen as his fingers flew across the keyboard. Mark didn't want to interrupt, but what he had was very important. "Kevin, my man. You got a minute?"

"Just a sec. I'm almost done here." His fingers tapped a little more on the keyboard as the light from the screen mirrored in his glasses. A rainbow of colors flashed in the reflection.

What in the world is he doing? Mark didn't want to sound impatient, but all the rushing colors made him wonder if Kevin was just playing around or what. *Let's take care of business, man.*

"Okay. Whatcha got?" Kevin pushed his glasses back up on his nose.

Mark passed the envelope to Kevin. "You remember that list of names you found from the various social networks Ken Richardson had tapped into? I need you to go through these. I highlighted ten names of interest. I'm hoping you can get me real names and addresses to go with the contact names. And I'm hoping some of these match up with the other list you gave me. I'm hoping we find some sort of pattern. I have his financials, so I'm going to double check that against what you find — if it appears to you buying and selling is for sure what is going on."

"That shouldn't be a problem." Kevin opened the envelope and slid the pages out.

"You'll notice a lot of strange conversations that I'm sure are similar to the conversations on the social networks. You know what I mean, where people will mean things other than what they are truly saying. Because what they are saying doesn't really make sense. At least I hope you find the same thing. I need a break . . . a lead . . . something."

"I'll get on it right now and call you as soon as I finish."

"Oh. One more thing. The one name highlighted in pink might be a love interest. See if you find anything that can confirm that — and who it is."

"Gotcha."

"Thanks, man. I appreciate your help." Mark gave a slight wave as he left Kevin's office.

Running down the stairs was a whole lot faster than jogging up, and easier. On the way back to his desk he took a second to pass by the break room and get a Coke. As he dropped the three quarters in the machine and pushed the button, he murmured, "Please, Lord. Open the door.

Point me in the right direction." He knew Ms. Cain's future depended on it, as well as her son's. A single mom raised Mark, and he knew how hard it was — but to be raised by a stranger would have to be worse. At least in his way of thinking it would.

A peace swept over him as he grabbed the soda can out of the machine drop. "Thanks," he whispered to the Lord.

With confidence he strode back into his office and plopped into his chair.

Ben looked up at the sound. His brows drew together, forming a deep V as he darted a glance in Mark's direction but said nothing. It was obvious that Ben wanted to know where all the confidence and vigor had suddenly come from. He wanted to know if Mark had found something that would drag him away from the trail Ben was running down full force.

But since the man truly didn't want to be redirected, he looked away quickly.

That worked for Mark, because he didn't want to tell Ben anything either — at least not yet.

CHAPTER 22

Sunday morning, as Sam's car curved around the lake following the two-lane road, she shivered.

"You should have worn a sweater. The weather is starting to cool." Margaret's voice was fueled with concern. "And I doubt the heater will be on in the sanctuary yet."

Sam nodded as she glanced in the rearview mirror. It wasn't the weather that left goose bumps lined up on Sam's arms, but dare she share her concern? A black SUV with dark tinted windows was behind her. SUVs were very popular, and although it had been said windows could only be so dark, it didn't stop people from going to the extreme. Seeing the vehicle shouldn't bother her, but for some reason it did. Was someone following her?

She turned right on Stanford Avenue and then left on Highland Road. When she glanced again, the same dark car stayed steady on her tail, about two car-lengths behind. She shrugged it off. She had to. Samantha didn't want to start suspecting everyone and everything. *Big deal.* So the black vehicle was going in the same direction as she was driving. They may even be going to the same church. That was what she told herself anyway. Her body didn't listen as her grip tightened on the steering wheel. Was it a coincidence?

To prove how silly she was being, instead of waiting until she got to Lee Drive to turn left, Sam decided to cut left a couple of blocks earlier on Stuart. Pinning a glance in the mirror, she didn't see the SUV behind her anymore. A quiet breath of relief seeped from her lips. *Great. They didn't follow us.*

"You okay, Momma?" Marty asked.

Straightening her back, she sat up in the seat and tucked some fine strands of hair behind her ear. "Sure, baby. I'm fine."

Margaret reached across the seat and patted her hands. "Relax. Things will get better. You know God's going to take care of you."

Glancing down at the steering wheel, she saw her knuckles. They were white from clenching the steering wheel. She loosened her grip and mouthed at Margaret, "Thank you."

A glance over her shoulder revealed Marty's worried eyes fixed on her.

"I'm okay, baby. Really I am. Smile and don't worry." *I just have an overactive imagination.*

Turning the car down a few more side roads, she made their way back to Lee Drive and then steered the car toward the side road of the church, directing the car to the parking lot behind it. When she stepped out of the car and shut the door, she heard the triple slam as each door closed simultaneously.

"See ya," Marty said as he dashed across the parking lot to the stairs that led up to his Sunday school class.

Taking a few extra seconds to look around, Sam double-checked, making sure it had all been her imagination working overtime.

"Sam, what's going on?" Margaret said from right next to her.

Sam jumped. She'd been concentrating so hard that she hadn't even noticed Margaret had walked around the car to join her.

"Your face is white like you've seen a ghost. And I saw a look of fear in your face as you were driving over here. You can talk to me, you know. Any time."

"Too many late-night movies, Margaret. You know me and my crime shows. It has my mind seeing things that don't exist." She tried to laugh at herself, but it came out weak.

"Shake it off and get into class then. You'll feel better after you spend some more time with the Lord and your fellow believers."

"You're right, Margaret." Sam couldn't help but grin. "And by the way, Greg said when we get into church to save him a seat. So if you get in there first, save three, not two, seats."

A slight blush touched Margaret's cheeks.

Their little romance seemed to be cultivating quite nicely, which made Sam happy. These were two people she loved very much, and the thought of them being attracted to each other made Sam's apprehensions slip to the back of her mind.

Margaret nodded and then went on to her class on the bottom floor, to the right of the stairs.

Glancing at her watch, Sam realized she needed to hurry or she would be late. She dashed across the parking lot and ran up the stairs. At the top, she peered out to the street one more time to reassure herself that it was only her imagination.

Instead, she caught a glimpse of a black SUV with dark-tinted windows rolling slowly down the side street of the church.

Was it the same one? She bit her bottom lip. The darkness of the tint on the windows confirmed it in her mind. It wasn't her imagination after all.

Why would someone be following her?

Detectives drove dark, plain, nondescript vehicles, and policemen drove cars with the bubbles on top and their name written everywhere in plain sight for all to see. Who would be following her in one of those big fancy SUVs where faces were hidden behind dark windows? In the movies, FBI and Special Forces drove those types of vehicles, but what would they be following her for? Her heart hammered.

Help me, Lord.

Almost three hours later, the four of them were sitting around the kitchen table chomping down on a pot roast Margaret had put in the slow cooker that morning before leaving for church. The wonderful fragrance of roast, onion, garlic, rosemary, green beans, and bacon peppered the air, keeping the focus on the food.

"If I keep eating like this, I'm going to gain twenty pounds in no time. I think I've already added an inch to my belt line. And it's entirely your fault, woman." He darted a light gaze in Margaret's direction, all the while a half smile etched his face. "You cook better than anyone I've ever known. Who can resist?"

Laughter surrounded the table as Marty said between laughs, "Oh, Uncle Greg, you haven't gotten fat. I know you're like Matthew. You work out all the time."

Suddenly a hush blanketed the air. It was the quick memory that quieted everyone, but Sam wanted it to be okay to talk about Matthew anytime.

The more, the better.

She loved him and wanted to always remember him. And she wanted the same for Marty. She didn't want her son to feel he had to watch what he said or for him to think talking or thinking about Matthew was a bad thing. No. It was a great thing, because Matthew was a great man who instilled a strong sense of courage into her young son.

A smile touched her lips. "You know, Marty. I think it's because Uncle Greg is working so hard tracking down the truth on Mr. Ken's death that he hasn't had time to do his daily exercises. You are right. When he does his normal routine like Matthew, Greg stays in great shape . . . for a man his age."

"Watch it!" Greg pointed his fork in Sam's

direction.

Chuckles filtered the air around the table.

"All I'm saying is you better look out, Greg. You and I both know Margaret's the best cook in the world. Right, Son?"

"Right."

"And pounds can slip on easily when you're not paying attention."

The older woman blushed as the compliments rained around her. "Eat up, people. The food is getting cold." She jabbed her fork in a piece of the meat and stuffed it in her mouth.

Sam noticed that Margaret's eyes softened as they rested on Greg. He filled his mouth with her cooking and then a satisfied look covered his face. Conversation and eating continued around the table. A nice family-feel filled Sam's heart as she soaked in the atmosphere.

After everyone finished and Margaret and Sam were clearing the dishes, the men went into the living room to relax and let their food settle while the women stayed behind to clean up the mess.

"Are you going to tell Greg about what happened this morning on the way to church? Tell him what you thought you saw? You never know. It may be important."

As Sam placed the leftover roast in a

plastic container and then poured the gravy over it, she said, "Yes. Unfortunately it is important. I'll tell you, too. I saw a big black SUV following us this morning — all the way to church." Popping the lid on top, she placed it in the refrigerator.

"Who would follow you?" Margaret rinsed the dishes as she started sticking them into the dishwasher.

Those were all the same questions Sam had already asked herself. She still had no answers, but maybe Greg would. When the table was clear and clean, Sam busied herself making a pot of coffee as Margaret finished filling the machine with the dirty dishes.

Within fifteen minutes they had the kitchen shining like new, and then they joined Greg and Marty in the living room. "Coffee will be ready in a minute or two."

Tom Sawyer and Huck Finn were keeping Marty entertained as everyone watched with him. Sam wasn't sure who laughed the hardest at some of their pranks, Marty or Greg.

When Margaret started to rise, Greg caught her arm and held her motionless. "I'll get it. You relax. I know how you take your coffee. Let me wait on you this time." His hand slid down her arm, and he gently held her hand for a moment.

Margaret rested back against the couch. A delighted smile touched her lips. "Thank you," she murmured.

He rose and jabbed a glance Sam's way. "I'm getting yours, too." His voice spoke with authority.

She smiled.

As he left the room, she stood and said, "I'll be back in a minute. Now's a good time to tell him," she whispered to Margaret, trying not to disturb Marty's concentration.

Pushing the door open, Sam stepped into the kitchen.

"I thought I told you, I got it," Greg said as he pulled three cups down from the cupboard. "What's the matter? You don't trust me?"

"Go right ahead and fix the cups of coffee. I'm here to watch. I love being waited on. There is no way I'm going to stop you." She grinned, but then let it fall. "I'm only here to talk."

A serious look crossed Greg's face. "What's the matter? Did something happen that I don't know about?"

Sam told him about her suspicious mind that morning. Then once she decided it was her imagination working tirelessly, unfortunately she saw the car again. "So who would be watching me? And why?"

"By the way you described the vehicle, it sounds like someone who doesn't want to be seen. I think of drug dealers . . . hardened criminals . . . killers. You know the kind of people I've dealt with over the years." Pouring the third cup, he continued sharing his thoughts aloud. "But what would any of them want with you? That's the question to ask. If it were the real killer, they wouldn't want to give any excuse to the police to start checking around for another suspect. I think it was coincidence. Don't dwell on it, but from now on, keep your eyes open for what is going on around you."

"So you don't think this SUV has anything to do with Ken's murder?"

"I didn't say that. I don't know. I hope not. It's like I said with the police already thinking you are the guilty party, why would anyone want to shift suspicion on them? They would be foolish. Right now the detectives think they have this case solved. The true killer wouldn't want to give them any cause to look elsewhere." Stirring all the cups, he grabbed one and handed it to Sam. "Here. You take yours."

"That makes sense." She took a sip of her coffee. Perfect. He did know how she liked it. The man paid attention. As she sipped the brew, Sam let his words sink in. Greg made sense, true, but if that was the case, why was someone following her this morning? She knew what she saw. And that didn't make sense. She sighed. "So Greg, what are we going to do next? Do you have a game plan for us?"

He picked up the other two cups. "Today is Sunday. We're going to take it easy. Tomorrow we'll start bright and early. You and I are going to go meet with an FBI agent I know. I'm hoping he can help us dig a little deeper into Ken's gambling. See if maybe Ken Richardson got in a little too deep with a bookie or two. And I have my friend in the corporate world checking on some of his under-the-table deals. See if any of them went sour," Greg said as he pushed the door open with his elbow and waited for Sam to enter the living room first.

"Thank you," she said as she passed him by.

Sam sat in Matthew's chair and leaned back. Pulling out the footrest on the recliner, she let her mind drift. Greg was right. Today was Sunday, the day of rest. Closing her eyes, she prayed, *Give us strength and direction for tomorrow, Lord. Lead us where You'd have us go.*

Her eyes popped open to a room full of

laughter. She glanced from one to the other and thought all was right with the world — at least, her little world.

She smiled.

Thank You, Lord.

CHAPTER 23

Sure it was his day off, but Mark knew today was a good day for him to accomplish his task without the watchful eye of his superior. With what all he discovered Friday, Ben seemed to keep a close watch on his partner. Maybe it was Mark who had an overactive imagination. Who knew? Maybe it was Mark's guilt talking to him, guilt of working behind his partner's back, but he felt certain Ben was trying to see if he could figure out what his partner was up to, at the same time working diligently on his own trail he was following.

Saturday another case had dropped into their laps, with the death of a white-collar worker. Was it suicide or murder? It wasn't uncommon to work more than one case at a time. Unfortunately that was the norm — to work several — due to the number of crimes versus the number of officers.

After following the leads in the death and

the evidence at the scene, both he and his partner felt certain it was suicide by the end of the day. Yes, there was a note, but that didn't always mean it was the real deal. However, everything pointed that way. There were a few loose ends they would tie up Monday, and then they could put that one to bed quickly.

Today he was going to follow the leads he had on the Richardson case. Hopefully one of them would pan out to be the one both he and his partner should be pursuing. But Mark had to get all the evidence, all the facts, before he could present it to his lieutenant.

The first thing he did was touch base with a friend of his, a narcotics agent. Jim met him at the precinct downtown where Jim was stationed when the man wasn't working undercover. At the station, the man always dressed clean, sharp, and neat. Undercover, you'd never know it was the same person.

Greetings were friendly, and after they caught up on one another's lives in a few sentences, they sat down at Jim's desk.

"These are the conversations I found texted on my victim's cell phone," Mark said as he handed a couple sheets of paper to his friend. "And these are from conversations Richardson had with other people in cyberspace. I found them on two different social media networks that Richardson frequented. And when my computer geek tracked the IP addresses, I found they led to two known users. I'm hoping this will help me find a reason for the man's death. Right now, the only direction this thing is going is this little piece of woman, an employee of his, a third his size, who supposedly killed the big guy without disturbing any furniture. No commotion whatsoever at the scene. We have it all: motive, means, and opportunity, but you really have to stretch the imagination to believe it's true."

Jim, interlacing his fingers, laid them behind his head as he rested back in his chair. "It's every cop's dream to have it laid out in front of him like that. Why are you so sure it's not true?"

"She was engaged to a fellow officer who always spoke highly of her. I find it hard to believe she could kill this big guy. Especially now that it seems he's involved with some very seedy characters. It makes more sense for it to be one of those guys. Besides, it's more circumstantial evidence against her than anything. I believe she's being set up."

Cocking his brow, Jim said, "You have to follow your gut. That's what makes a good cop — One who follows his instincts as well as the evidence. Let me look at this." Jim reached out and took the pages Mark had handed to him and started scanning them.

"I found Richardson's bank statements reflected some set patterns that coincided with the texting. The day before the person texting Richardson, the one highlighted in orange, met him, Richardson had removed a large sum of money from his account. A week after the texting from other parties, conversations marked in blue, I found large deposits made to Richardson's account — totaling almost double what he withdrew the week prior. Same with the social media notes. Looks like he's dealing to me. I thought with the names I have for you, you might be able to shed some light on the matter for me. Hopefully confirming my suspicions."

The pages drew Jim's undivided attention. After he studied the names and conversations, and looked at the connection with the bank statements, he asked, "Do you have a picture of your victim?"

Mark had brought his complete folder with him. Digging through it, he pulled out a single sheet. "Here's a good one."

Nodding, Jim said, "I've seen him with the biggest distributor we have in the city, but my guy wouldn't do business with him.

Look what he missed out on." Handing back the papers, he said, "I think you're on to something. But the question you have to ask yourself is if he's selling, making money for the big dealer, why would the head of the drug ring want to off his money train?"

Mark sat back and blew out a gush of air. Jim was right. Why would anyone making money from the chump want to kill him? He raked his fingers through his tight curls of brown hair. "Thanks. I didn't think of it that way. I just know the woman we're chasing for the crime isn't the killer. I have to find the right trail to follow." Stuffing the papers back into his file, he closed it, and then extended his hand.

As Jim shook it, Mark said, "I appreciate your time and your insight."

"No problem, Barnett. But I didn't say don't look in that direction. There are reasons people kill people in the drug business every day. They may not make sense to us, but drug users don't always think. They are too focused on their next score. And drug dealers . . . it's all about the money. Maybe Richardson shorted his supplier. Maybe one of Richardson's buyers came up short and thought it was easier to off his dealer than come up with the money he owed him. Either way, there are always reasons. Good luck on finding your perp."

Mark climbed back into his black pickup and headed to his apartment. Turning the music up loud on his radio still didn't wash away all his doubts.

What if he couldn't find another suspect? What if she did it, like Ben thought? Why did Mark believe so strongly in her innocence? What was it to him?

All those questions raced through his mind. But no matter how many questions hit him, he knew down deep in his gut that Samantha Cain was innocent.

Help me, Lord. Help me find the true guilty party. Don't let an innocent woman take the blame.

CHAPTER 24

The first thing Monday morning, Sam and Greg talked with Todd Holmes, Greg's friend from the Bureau. He had the intel on the top controllers of the big gambling rings. Unfortunately, Ken Richardson was only involved in a small way. The man was addicted to gambling — on everything. But in the insignificant ways he gambled, no one officially bothered to look at him twice.

Todd gave Greg a list of bookies. "One may have been Richardson's, but unless the man didn't pay up after a loss, they wouldn't be going after him. And if he was a regular who paid when he lost, they definitely wouldn't want to kill him. Break his leg, maybe, if he was late paying up, but that wasn't the way things played out in today's world. Bookies got their money, and as long as their customer found ways to pay off their debts, everyone was happy. In fact, they loved losers who could pay. That was how they made their fortunes."

They thanked Todd for his time and headed to the car.

"I'm sorry this lead didn't pan out," Greg said as he opened the door for Samantha. "But the good thing is, we can cross off the gambling addiction as a motive and focus on his bad work ethics."

Sam's shoulders sagged.

Slamming the door closed after she got in, he walked around to the drivers' side. As he climbed in, Sam said, "Are we ever going to find out who set me up?"

Silence was Greg's response. What could he say? Of course he planned to find this guy, whatever it took. She knew that, but waiting and wondering was wearing her down.

"I don't understand why I was picked as the patsy. Ken and I were never close, so why me?"

Greg reached across the front seat and covered her hand with his. "Because you do have a connection to the man through work, and apparently the killer knew of the discord between the two of you."

"Whoa. Then that raises another question." Her voice grew in volume as the questions mounted. "How can they know about me, when I don't know about them?" She scratched her head for a split second. "I don't get it."

Pinning his eyes briefly on Samantha, he returned his gaze to the road in front of him and deliberated. "That's a good question. Maybe it's something we need to look at a little closer." As he kept the car between the lines and continued toward Sam's home, he said, "We need to make a new list. We'll work on it as soon as we get to your house."

Sam sat up taller in her seat. She thought she heard a glimmer of hope in his voice. "What are you thinking?"

"Let's make the list and then I'll tell you. Your words just gave me a thought, one I should have thought before now." He glanced her way again, this time with a big grin.

Back at the house, they gathered around the kitchen table one more time. Margaret brought the cups of coffee and Sam pulled out a notepad. Opening it, she flipped pages until she found a fresh sheet. "Okay. What kind of list are we making this time?" Sam asked as Margaret set a cup before each of them.

"I want you to think hard. List everyone you know who also knows Ken."

"That's easy, but it will take forever to write. Everyone who works for Bulk, all across the nation. It's a long list." She laughed, her disappointment filtering through her tone as she dropped the pen on top of the tablet. "I don't think I even want to go there."

He shook his head. "No. No. We know you both know all the employees at your company. I'm talking about outside the company. Don't even list names from other businesses connected to Bulk that you two know in common. I want names away from the trucking industry."

She straightened her spine as she sat up in her chair. "Humph." Her brows lifted. "Sounds like you've come up with something, even though I don't get it." Lifting her cup, she took a sip of the dark brew, then set her cup back down. "That will be a short list." Lifting the pen back up, her hand hovered over the blank page as she thought.

"As long as it's complete."

Margaret's eyes sparkled. "Oh Greg. It sounds like you have an idea who killed Ken Richardson."

Greg reached over the table and laid his hand on top of Margaret's. "I do believe I might. Not the person, mind you, but the type of person we may be looking for. Let's just see who she lists."

The older woman turned her hand up and

cupped his, then squeezed.

Sam could feel the excitement in the air. She hoped she had the answer, the right name. A few names flittered through her mind. Snapping the button on top of the pen, exposing the point with ink, she touched it to the paper and started scribbling.

The only names she could come up with were his two best friends, who she knew but not well, and then his wife and his mother. She started to list his children but then scratched that idea. Truly she knew of them, not the girls themselves. She'd only known them by what Ken had said about them in passing and that was in the early days of his employment, when Sam was on the day shift. She tried to think of any other name she could add to the list, but drew a blank. "I don't know how this will help, but here you go." She tore the piece of paper from the tablet and handed it to Greg. "The names listed are all people who cared about Ken and barely knew me at all."

His eyes scanned the short list and the smile returned. "That's what I thought. If it's not work-related, or gambling-related, it's like what you said. It had to be someone who knew the bad vibes between the two of you. Someone personal. Who better than his best friends or his wife? We need to look closer at them. I know they seemed helpful when we talked in the beginning, against better judgment I suspect, but that could have been a front so they wouldn't be suspected."

His friends seemed helpful, maybe, but Dorothy didn't seem one way or the other. It has to be one of his friends. How could she not have thought of that before? His buddy from Arkansas, the one who flirted on the phone with her when he called to find out where his buddy was that night . . . to see if she knew. Timothy Tyler.

"Greg, I know we talked to his fishing buddy, Jerry Connors, who lives here. But we never talked to Timothy Tyler, his friend from his hometown. They grew up together. I know they live over a thousand miles apart, but they've been friends for over fifty years. I know they used to talk all the time. Every year they took a vacation together. Could they have had a falling out? He has called several times over the past few months asking me what Ken was up to, like I would know. At the time, I always thought it was because maybe Ken didn't answer a call and Timothy assumed he was called out to an accident somewhere, or I'd called him to the terminal for a problem."

"I had talked to him before, but only a very short conversation that at the time seemed forthwith, but I think all three make great candidates. In fact, I think we should start with his wife."

"What?" Sam shook her head. "I don't think so. There is no way Dorothy could have killed Ken. She's smaller than me. Besides, she loves the man." A chill swept her body from head to toe. "How could anyone find that man loveable?"

"You *think* she does, and maybe she does. But people don't always know what goes on behind closed doors. Besides, usually that is the first place police look and no one has looked that way as far as I know. I know we didn't. So it needs to be looked at."

Sam sighed. Her head was pounding. If that was standard procedure to police, they probably checked Dorothy out quickly and then moved on to Sam because they couldn't find anything. She couldn't believe Dorothy had anything to do with Ken's death. It just wasn't in her nature. And then to blame it on Sam? No. Not Dorothy. Sam rubbed her temples, trying to chase away the headache.

"It's okay, sweetie," Margaret said gently. "Nothing makes sense. But Greg knows what he's doing. You should trust him."

Dropping her hands to the table, she nodded slightly. "I do trust him. I just know Dorothy, and I can't believe she would do this to him or to me."

Greg finished his coffee and set his cup back down. "If you're that sure, we'll start with," he looked at the list and then said, "Timothy and Jerry first. Do you know what town Timothy's from? Where he lives now? Do you know if he and Ken have been together lately? And are Jerry and Timothy friends? Do they know one another? Jerry was helpful, but it could have been a front."

"I don't know. I can only remember Timothy coming to town maybe twice. Usually Ken and Dorothy went up there." Sam wrote down the name of the city Ken and Timothy were from. Other than Timothy's name and the town he lived in, Sam didn't know much about the man. Over the few years Ken had been her boss, she had only talked to him on the phone maybe ten times a year tops, if that many. Usually the man joked about his friend and always made Sam laugh. She remembered thinking, why couldn't her boss be as nice to her as he was? But it never changed anything between her and her boss. Ken probably didn't know that Timothy was so nice to her over the phone. He would have stopped it, I'm sure.

Who knows? Maybe Ken never told Timothy about the problems between the two of them.

"Greg, I just had a thought. Maybe Timothy didn't know about our conflicts. Maybe Ken never talked about me to the man." She explained to him quickly the thoughts that had just crossed her mind. "To him, our indifferences were of no consequence, so why would he even think about me when he was hanging out or talking with his best friend?"

"It's possible Ken never mentioned the rift between the two of you, but some men like to talk about women — especially if they have a power over them. Some even like to embellish on their relationships, even when there isn't one. He probably enjoyed putting you down to his buddy, and he probably bragged about the power he held over you. It's a man thing. Not a good thing, mind you, but people like Ken Richardson enjoy bragging about a sense of power they feel they have. It's a control issue, as well as an ego booster."

"What about his kids? Didn't you know them, too?" Margaret asked. "You talked about the way they reacted when you showed up to pay your respects, and it sounded like you knew them. Or at least they knew you."

"I know of them, but I don't know them personally. I'd only met the youngest daughter once and knew of the three girls from when Ken bragged on them to me. It happened sometimes, but not often. He didn't share his personal life with me or with any of us for that matter."

Finishing her last swallow, Margaret asked, "Can I fix either of you another cup? I'm about to make tuna salad for lunch. Greg, would you like to join us?"

He darted a grin her way. "I'd love to, but I'll have to pass this time, Darlin'. I'm going to go see what I can dig up on Timothy Tyler and Jerry Connors. Thanks for asking."

After Greg left, the girls made the tuna salad then sat down to enjoy a bite together. Margaret talked up a storm about Marty. Sam knew it was an attempt on Margaret's part to keep Sam's mind off of the trouble at hand, and she was grateful for it.

When lunch was over and their little mess cleaned up, Margaret said, "I'm going to take a trip to the store. We're out of milk and a few other items. Can you think of anything you'd like me to pick up for you while I'm out?"

Sam thought for a second but couldn't

come up with anything.

About five minutes after Margaret left, Sam picked up her Bible. She stepped into the living room and looked out of the big picture window. Memories flashed of times before. She would stand looking out and Matthew would come up behind her, holding her. Memories of watching the sparkles flashing across the lake as he held her in his arms. That brought more peace and serenity to her than one could fathom. She sighed. With Bible in hand, she turned and padded to what was now her favorite chair — Matthew's.

Quietness filled the house like Sam had never heard. At times the sounds of silence could be deafening, but right now it was welcomed. Reading the Word helped the tension flow out of her, relaxing her. She let the stress of life slip off her shoulders as she closed her eyes and bowed her head. Taking time to thank the Lord for all her blessings, she then asked him to continue to direct their path in this investigation. She admitted to the Lord she had no idea as to how to bring the guilty party to justice, but she also knew from His Word that was what He did.

Vengeance is mine, saith the Lord.

When she finished her prayer, she thought

aloud, "I don't want vengeance. I only want the guilty to be brought to justice. And that is what the Lord does." As she spoke those words, she reminded herself to leave it in His mighty and capable hands.

Breathing a sigh of relief, she started to relax as the phone pealed out a loud ring in the silent house. She jumped, then chuckled to herself for being so silly.

"It's only the phone ringing," she scolded herself as she rose to answer it.

Stepping near the sofa she reached for the receiver. Pulling it to her ear, in a soft voice, she said, "Hello."

"Samantha. Hi. It's me, Dorothy. I know you haven't been able to work lately so I felt sure you didn't know about the arrangements I made for Ken's funeral."

"Hi, Dorothy. Thank you for calling. You're so right. No one has told me anything lately. Everyone seems to be staying as far away from me as possible. I'm taboo. I have to admit your call surprises me. I hope this means you know I didn't do it."

"Of course, dear. I never believed you had anything to do with it from the beginning. I'm so sorry that one of those detectives seems so bent on pinning it on you."

"That means so much to me, Dorothy.

Thank you." A heaviness lifted off of Sam's shoulders. Had she been that downtrodden? Apparently so, and now relief gently invaded her heart.

"Samantha, you are the sweetest person I've ever met. I know Ken rode you hard. That was something I never understood, except maybe because you are a woman. Anyway, I know you wouldn't have done such a thing." The female voice sounded friendly to her ears.

"I wish the police felt the same way. I would have never hurt Ken." Sam wrapped the telephone cord connecting the receiver to the phone around her finger and then let it loose again. Freedom filled her heart, as Dorothy sounded so reassuring, believing in Sam's innocence.

"I know, dear. I've expressed to the police I felt they were way off track going after you, but they didn't want to listen to me."

Jones, she thought. "Sorry your kids don't feel the same way you do. Your girls believe what the police are saying, so they think I'm a killer. I felt the tension when I stopped by. I'm so sorry."

"As for my kids, I've tried to reassure them as well, but that's their daddy, and they don't want to hear me defending the person the police think is guilty, so I can't say much. Anyway, I wanted to tell you the arrangements have been made. You may or may not want to come to the wake, but I'm sure if you want to make it to the funeral itself, and watch him being lowered in the ground, surely everyone would understand. After all, you've worked for the man several years."

Sam frowned but didn't say a word. Surely she would look more guilty if she only showed up to watch him being buried. It would be like she wanted to make sure the man was dead and gone.

A chill swept over her.

"Aahh . . ." She tried to think of the right words to say, but nothing came to mind.

"Are you okay, Sam? I didn't call to upset you, dear. I know your life is in a mess and, after last year, that serial killer, and then Matthew's death, I wouldn't think this would be easy to bear. Is someone with you? You don't need to be alone."

"No. No one is here at the moment, but Margaret won't be gone too long. I'm okay. Thanks for caring. It's I who should be offering aid to you, Dorothy. If there is anything I can do, please don't hesitate to ask me. I'm here for you."

Dorothy conveyed the details of the arrangements, and then they said their good-byes.

Sam sat back down in Matthew's chair and clutched her Bible to her chest. "Thank You, Lord for helping Dorothy realize that I didn't kill her husband." She lay back in the chair and closed her eyes, waiting for that peace to overtake her again.

But it never came.

CHAPTER 25

Mark whipped his truck into the parking lot of the station. Disappointment consumed him. How could he not find the killer? He just knew it had something to do with the man's dealing drugs. All the signs were there. All the coded messages and texts. The money trail proved the man was dirty, but it didn't lead him to the killer.

Jamming the gears into park, he jumped out of his truck with his file in hand and dragged himself into the precinct. He always found his desk a great place to think, especially when he and Ben were on the same trail. They would bounce ideas off one another. It worked. Just not now, because Ben had his mind made up, and there was no changing it.

Mark hauled himself to his desk, dropped the file on it, and plopped down in his chair. For days now he had been going over and over his file, but to no avail. Lacing his fingers behind his head, he leaned back and closed his eyes. *What now?*

Flipping his file open one more time, he wanted to look anew, hoping something would pop out. As he glanced over the report of the first policeman at the scene, he heard the door of the homicide division open. He felt a tight squeeze on his heart as he believed Ben had just walked in the door. Any minute he'd find out what Mark had been up to, yet he still had nothing concrete.

Turning slightly as he looked up, Mark's eyes spread in surprise. It wasn't Ben.

"Can I help you?" Mark asked.

"I sure hope so," said the other man who also believed in Samantha Cain's innocence. "Can we talk?"

"Have a seat," Mark said reluctantly. "Greg, is it?"

Should he discuss this ongoing case with an ex-cop? A man who believed the opposite of what his partner believed. Should he? Maybe this was what he needed to do. Maybe the two of them could bounce ideas back and forth. The beating of Mark's heart started to race.

Hold on, boy.

He had to slow himself down here. He was getting ahead of himself. Let him see what the man had to say.

"Greg Singleton," he said as he sat. "I've been doing a little investigating on my own. First, I want you to know Samantha Cain does not know that I am here. I hope I'm making the right choice. When I left her house this afternoon and was heading home to follow up on a few new ideas, your face flashed through my mind. When it did, I took a chance coming by here, hoping to find you."

"Well, it's your lucky day. I don't usually work on Sundays and Mondays, but I happened by here a short time ago. What do you need?"

"I need to prove to you Samantha Cain is innocent." Greg's fist pounded Mark's desktop.

"Hold on, buddy. Don't get all riled up on me. First, I have to admit, I believe she is innocent also."

Shaking his head, Greg's fist relaxed. "I knew it. I knew it. You are nothing like your partner. I believe I can talk to you. Trust you to listen. Trust you to do the right thing."

Sticking his right hand up in the air, palm facing the man at his desk, Mark said, "Don't get carried away here, man. Know whatever you share with me, I will be sharing with my partner if I feel it is pertinent to the case."

Clearing his throat, Greg said, "No problem. I'm not asking you to keep secrets. In fact, I believe if I can tell you what I've found, maybe it will help you two find the real killer . . . that is, if you are looking past Sam."

"I can't discuss an ongoing case with you. You're free to tell me what you've found out, but don't expect me to share with you what we know. You were a cop. You know how this works." Mark quietly, and hopefully unobtrusively, closed the open file on his desk. He didn't know if the man knew how to read upside down or what. Cops always had their own specialties. Right now Mark was open to hearing what Greg had to say, but not so ready to spill his thoughts to the man. His partner would never understand. And Mark didn't want to do or say anything that would jeopardize the case.

Greg pulled a little notepad from his pocket and flipped through some pages. "We've been talking to people who work or worked with Ken Richardson, trying to find out more about the man himself."

Mark nodded but didn't interrupt. That was what he had tried to get his partner to do; so right now this guy seemed to be going in the direction Mark believed the case should go . . . looking into the victim.

"We've found out that Ken Richardson wasn't quite the innocent man everyone tried to picture him to be. Sure, he and Sam never got along and all the evidence at the crime scene looks to be pointing in her direction, but to any good cop, which I believe you are, they would see it was a setup."

"Possible setup," Mark said in a correcting tone. His thoughts exactly, but again he didn't want to share that with Greg Singleton.

"Right. In talking with ex-employees and coworkers and even some people at the plants the company worked with, we found out some interesting things about Ken Richardson."

"I'm sure you did, but the question is, are the things you found out fact or opinion?" Mark wanted to hear him out, but he wanted the facts, not supposition. He had enough of those on his own.

"Facts. I checked some of this out with some official people I can still talk with. At the present, I don't want to name names. I'd rather just tell you what I have. What we have."

"You and Ms. Cain?"

"Yes."

"I'm still listening. Try to get to the point. This is my off day, if you don't mind." Mark didn't dare tell him he was spending his off day trying to prove her innocence. If the man had something, Mark wanted to hear it, and he needed him to spit it out.

"Richardson did some under-the-table deals. Some of them or one of them could have gotten him killed. Also the man was addicted to gambling, which could also put his life in jeopardy."

"All of this still sounds like supposition to me," Mark said. "I love all the hypotheses you're sharing with me, but what facts do you have?"

Greg sat forward in his chair and leaned in the detective's direction. "We know for a fact he was in to all of these things and we believe one of these things got him killed. He was a dishonest man. Dishonest people get caught, make wrong choices all the time, and things backfire. I have plans to talk some more to his two best friends because I believe they know more about the man than anyone. And I'm hoping they will tell me. Who knows? Maybe he shafted his best friend and then he had him killed. I don't know. The only thing I do know is Samantha Cain is innocent and if you two don't start chasing the right leads, you'll never find the truth." On those words, with chest puffed up, Greg stood. His eyes bore down on Mark.

"Sit back down, Mr. Singleton."

After a moment, the man did as he was told.

"Truth be told, I believe Samantha Cain is innocent also. I'm here today trying to find the one piece we are missing." Mark didn't mean to open his mouth to this man, but once he started, he couldn't stop. "Something has bothered me from the get-go, and I can't seem to bring what it is to the front of my mind. I was hoping one of your facts would do that — joggle it loose, but it didn't. I know Matthew Jefferies believed in Samantha Cain, and that was enough in the beginning for me not to believe everything my partner said. Unfortunately he was one of those police-men who believed she got away with murder. He believed she killed Martin Cain, her husband, years back. He keeps saying people don't change."

Greg shrugged and then nodded. "I believe people don't change easily. I believe situations change people. I just don't know enough of the facts on the case to know who is the guilty party. I do know it's not Sa-mantha. I've even found proof of infidelity on Ken Richardson's part." Pulling his pad out of his pocket, Greg flipped a couple of pages over and then said, "Elizabeth Brumfield. Lizzie to her friends. Did y'all ever check out the wife? Did y'all find out if she knew anything about his girlfriend? Usually the spouse is the first person of interest, and the first to know when a husband is fooling around."

Instantly, something shot through Mark's mind, and he turned over the file cover, exposing the first report in the folder. Was it that simple?

The first policeman on the scene stated something in his file that pricked at Mark's brain. Using his pointer finger as a guide, he scanned down the report. Flipping the first page over, he came to the notification of next-of-kin. Jabbing his finger on the paper, he said, "That's it!" He smiled at Greg.

"What's it?"

"That was what bothered me from the get-go. When Mrs. Richardson was told about her husband's death, she told the officer Samantha Cain had called at midnight. Said he was needed at the terminal right away. And when we questioned Ms. Cain, she said she never called him. That should have thrown up red flags all around for us, but for some reason it was pushed to the side."

"Because your partner didn't want to hear the truth."

"Don't go there, Mr. Singleton. Let's stay on track here. If Samantha never called at midnight, the question is, who did?" Mark flipped the pages over in his file until he came to the phone records. Glancing at the records of the office phone, he saw there was no call made to Ken Richardson's home or cell phone at midnight. Just like Ms. Cain said, but she could have used her cell phone. Quickly, he flipped a few more pages over and glanced at Ken Richardson's home phone. He found one incoming call at midnight and jotted down the number.

"What did you find? I see you are on to something. Can you tell me?"

"Hold on, Mr. Singleton." Mark flipped through the home calls, seeing if that number had called before. No such thing. Next he glanced through the phone calls to Richardson's cell phone. There it was. Fifteen minutes long. Again, five minutes. Again and again. He kept finding a repeat of that same number calling. Each day there were a couple or more incoming or outgoing calls to that number, and each time it lasted from five minutes up to thirty. This was someone they needed to talk to. They, as in his partner and himself. But would Ben follow up with him? Should he go by himself? It was always best to have backup. This could be the killer.

Mark glanced at Greg Singleton. *Take him with you.* Blowing out a spurt of air but shaking his head, Mark said, "Okay. We're going to go for a quick ride . . . if you want to go with me. It's sort of your lead, so I'm inviting you — but not officially. You are not a policeman."

"I do carry a gun, you know. I work to protect the governor."

Mark nodded. "I know. I checked into you. That's why I'm making this offer to you." He punched a couple of keys on his computer, typed in the phone number, and then jotted down the name, Elizabeth Brumfield, and her address. Tearing the top page off of his notepad, he rose to his feet. "It looks like your suspicions may be true. Are you coming?"

"You couldn't leave me here if you tried."

That was what Mark was hoping he would say. As much as he hated doing this without his partner, as long as they got to the truth, he felt sure in the end Ben would understand and agree with him. Right now, his partner was wearing blinders so thick he couldn't see the forest for the trees, as the old saying went. But Mark knew the older detective was a good cop, and in the end he would want true justice.

"Let's go."

CHAPTER 26

The doorbell rang, and Sam's eyes popped open. Who could that be?

Laying her Bible on the end table, she rose. As she stepped toward the door, her eyes glanced toward the window, hoping to recognize the car. Nothing she could see in the driveway. Well, she knew it wasn't the detectives. They would have pounded on the door. That was Jones' way of announcing himself.

The bell rang a second time as her hand reached the doorknob. Opening the door slightly, she was surprised. "Dorothy! Come in," she invited. "I didn't know you were so close when we were on the phone a few minutes ago."

"Yes, dear. I realized it only moments ago myself and thought, why not stop by? You sounded so distraught. I wanted to come cheer you up." Her sweet words practically embraced Samantha as Dorothy entered the living room.

"Thank you so much. It's so sweet of you to be thinking of me at a time like this. It's I who should be there for you. Let's go in the kitchen, and I'll fix us some coffee. You do drink coffee, don't you?"

"I'd love a cup," her voice rang out. "Thanks."

After closing and locking the front door, Sam led the way to the kitchen. Dorothy followed closely on her heels.

"Has your housekeeper made it home yet? I know Marty won't be home from school for a couple more hours."

Sam slowed in her steps as she noticed a slight shift in Dorothy's tone. Turning, she glanced at her guest, and the woman flashed a sweet smile in her direction. It must have been Sam's imagination.

"Margaret is so much more than a housekeeper," she said. "Over the past year she has become more like family than anything." Sam pushed the swinging door and stepped through to the kitchen.

Dorothy followed. "That's wonderful. Does she live with you all the time?"

"As a matter of fact, she does." Stepping to the cupboard, Sam opened the door and took down two cups. Glancing at the pot, she saw it was practically empty. "I'll make a fresh pot. Do you have enough time?"

Her guest didn't answer, so she turned toward Dorothy and froze in her step, almost dropping the empty cups.

"Sit down." The command came in a deep, angry voice, and the strength came from the gun pointing in Sam's direction. "Now."

Keeping her eyes on the gun, Sam set the cups on the counter and then pulled out a chair. Quickly she slid into it. "What's going on, Dorothy?" *I thought she believed me. Why is she doing this?* The look in the woman's eyes brought chills to Sam. Icy fingers played havoc with her neck and shoulders and then slid down her back. "Why are you doing this?"

"You should already be in jail for killing Ken," Dorothy spat at her.

"But I didn't do it. I thought you believed me?" Sam's heart broke, seeing so much pain in Dorothy's face.

Waving the gun in Sam's direction, Dorothy said, "Don't be so stupid, girl. I know you didn't do it — but you were supposed to be blamed for it. Everything pointed toward you. Why are you not in jail?"

Sam wasn't sure how to answer that, or even if she was supposed to answer Dorothy. She seemed to be more talking out loud to herself than she was to Sam.

"I had it all worked out. Everything was going as planned. You should have already been arrested, case closed, and Ken buried. But no. You're still running around free, asking questions, visiting *my* home, and upsetting *my* girls. I can't let this go on. They were trying to figure out a way to take revenge on you. I don't want my kids to end up in jail because their father was a no-good piece of garbage."

Dorothy's eyes stared straight at Sam, but the woman seemed to be miles away.

Her girls planned to harm me? Sam couldn't believe it. "What are you saying?"

"I'm saying you've ruined everything. I can't let my girls kill you, thinking you killed their precious father. They would end up in jail, and with the way they are feeling now, they don't care. But I do."

Sam wished she knew what she should do. Call the police, of course. But how could she? The woman had a gun on her. Greg wouldn't be coming back over today. He was gone until tomorrow. And Margaret, Sam had no idea how long she would be gone to the store. She definitely didn't want Dorothy to still be here when Margaret got home. The woman was acting crazy. She could hurt her. Sam couldn't be responsible for that. She had to figure out a way out of this.

"What do you want, Dorothy? How can I help you?"

"If you only knew. My husband used to come home complaining about the snip of a girl who worked a man's job, who thought she knew so much. He hated you. I could tell. He hates strong women. He likes women to be submissive to their man, in every way. I was his doormat for so many years, I was sick of it. His little girlfriend was the last straw." Shaking her head, she said, "I have to go to plan B. I wasn't going to do this. But it's the only way. If they would have arrested you, you could have gone to jail and maybe got a light sentence because of the way he treated you. You could have said you snapped. Everyone knew. You have so many friends at that company they would have all come to sweet Samantha's aid."

Plan B? What was plan B? Surely the woman wasn't going to just shoot her. Then the police would know something wasn't right. *Think. Think. What can you do to distract her and get to the phone?*

"Get a pen and paper. Now!"

Sam scooted out her chair and stepped over to the junk drawer. Pulling it open, she grabbed the little notepad she had used to write possible suspects on for Greg. The one name she didn't want to put on it turned out to be the one who did it. But how? Dorothy was smaller than Sam.

She grabbed a pen and sat back down at the table. "What are you doing, Dorothy? You know I didn't do it, so tell me. Who did?"

"No one you know. I hired someone. A professional."

"You hated him that much?" Sam truly felt sorry for the woman.

"Look who's talking. You hated my husband, too."

"But I —"

"Shut up. I want you to write a letter to your son. Tell him how sorry you are for having to leave him. Tell him you couldn't live with the guilt. However you want to say it. Remember, it will be the last chance you have to talk to your son."

"This is crazy!"

"Do it!"

Dear Lord. Help me out of this. What do I do?

"Start writing, or I'll write it for you. I'll print. No one would be the wiser."

Drawing in a deep breath, she glanced at the gun and then at Dorothy. "I'll write him a note, but tell me what you plan to do."

"Don't be so foolish. I plan to kill you, of course," Dorothy said, as if it were the only natural thing to do.

Sam tried to think of ways to stall her. But when she glanced at Dorothy again, she noticed the woman's hand was starting to shake. That gun could go off by accident if she wasn't careful.

Pretending to start writing, Sam looked down and scribbled slowly on the paper. "You know, no one is going to believe that I killed myself here and left a mess for my son to come home and find me dead on the floor. I've been too much of a loving mother. Everyone will know something else happened —"

A ringing phone interrupted Sam. Automatically she rose to go answer the phone.

"Sit down. Let it ring. I need to think, but I know I'm not going to let you talk on the phone." The ringing continued. "Keep writing. Finish the note to your son. Remember, it's your last words to him so you better make them count."

On the fifth ring the machine picked up. As usual, the sound was turned down, so Sam had no idea who was calling or what was being left on the machine for her. Would she ever get to hear it? Would she ever get to see her son again? Would Dorothy have enough decency in her not to leave Sam dead on the floor for her son to find? That would scar him for life.

Finally, to be safe, she did write something on the paper. She wrote, *I'll always love you, Marty. Forgive me.* Dropping the pen on the table, she rose, shoving the chair back with her legs. It screeched across the floor. "I'm finished. Please don't kill me here."

"Toss me the paper. I want to read it for myself."

Sam shoved the tablet across the table. Turning it around, Dorothy glanced down at it but kept the gun aimed on Samantha. "Ah. How sweet. Yes, this is perfect. Where is your car? I think it would be for the best if I take you away from here to do this. You're right. No one would believe you'd kill yourself and leave it for your boy to find. I'm glad you're thinking."

"My car is in the carport, out back."

"All right. Grab your key and let's go. You first."

Sam moved over to the counter quickly and Dorothy hollered, "Slow steps. I'm watching you, and I will shoot you here if need be."

Moving slower, Sam grabbed her key ring

off of the counter and held it up for Dorothy's inspection, then slowly made her way toward the back door. She could hear her killer's feet shuffling in her direction, closing the gap between them.

Suddenly the swinging door flew open. A scream filled the air as a gun fired.

"Margaret!" Sam cried out as she turned toward the door.

CHAPTER 27

Lizzie spilled her guts in no time. She talked about her affair with Ken Richardson. She stated everything was going well — until this big threatening man who knew of the affair approached her. Someone she didn't name, but she revealed his threat. "The only way to protect myself was by following his orders. I didn't know he was going to kill Ken."

Mark couldn't believe how quickly she gave herself up.

"The man was going to kill me," she cried. "I had to do it. I had no other choice. Then I had to keep my mouth shut. It was the only way to stay alive!"

"You have the right to remain silent. Use it." Mark had a squad car coming to pick up Elizabeth Brumfield for accessory to murder. The woman couldn't give him the name of the one who did the actual killing. Mark needed that man to identify who hired the killer. But the way Lizzie described the killer, he sounded like a professional hit man. If he was, why didn't he kill Lizzie after she did what he needed her to do? *Surely she could recognize him, if we ever brought him in for questioning, which is exactly what we plan to do.*

Shaking his head, the truth hit Mark in the face. The killer was a professional. The man only killed whom they paid him for — a sick man, but a lucky break for Lizzie. The pro must already be out of the country. So now Mark needed to discover who hired him. It had to be Mrs. Richardson, because of the girl. Why else use her?

When the squad car arrived and took Lizzie out in handcuffs, Mark said, "At least now I can go to Ben, and he'll have to believe Samantha is innocent. Maybe he'll figure out a way to catch Mrs. Richardson for hiring a hit man."

They followed the policeman out the door.

"I know y'all will get the true killer now." He pulled his phone out of his pocket, hit a button and pressed the phone to his ear.

"Who are you calling? Do you know something I don't?"

"I'm calling Sam. She has a right to know. It's going to break her heart to find out it's probably Dorothy Richardson who killed her husband. Sam just knew she was innocent."

Mark shook his head. "Usually it's the one you least expect. Glad that it didn't turn out to be Ms. Cain."

Greg snapped his phone shut. "I knew it wasn't."

"No answer?"

"No. And I know she's home, unless she and Margaret went by the store. She lives just a few blocks from here. Would you mind us rolling by there so I can tell her right away? Or better yet, you tell her. I'm sure she'd love to hear it from you. It would be more believable. From me she'd think it was wishful talking."

Mark nodded. "No problem. I'd love to bring that woman some good news for a change."

They got into the car and Mark fired up the engine.

"I'm glad I was led to your door, to trust you'd do the right thing."

"I'm glad you were willing to share your findings with me," Mark said. "It helped unlock what was stuck in my mind and wouldn't come out. Have you ever had a case like that, where you knew something was important and it was staring you in the face, but you couldn't get it to come to the forefront?"

Greg chuckled. "I sure don't miss those days. Trying to solve a crime can give you ulcers, so be careful, lad."

Mark turned the wheel and into the drive. "You know it's a passion . . . a calling. You were a cop, so you know what I'm talking about."

As the car came to a stop, Greg climbed out. Mark was right behind him as they headed up the sidewalk to the front door. Suddenly a scream pierced the air, and a gun went off. Both took off into a run and rushed up the steps. Turning the knob, Mark hoped the door was unlocked. It was, so they both rushed in. The commotion was going on in the kitchen, and the swinging door was barely swinging. Greg caught Mark by the arm, the one not holding a gun already extended and ready for action.

Mark turned his gaze on the older man and watched him motion with his hands. Understanding, he moved slowly toward the swinging door as Greg shot around in the other direction, but moving ever so quietly.

As Mark eased up to the kitchen door, he heard a woman say, "You shot her. Let me help her."

"You just keep heading toward the back door. We're going for a little ride. They'll think you shot her. I'm not worried about her."

Sam watched as Dorothy stepped around Margaret's body, moving closer to Samantha. Using her gun, she motioned for Sam to move. Out of the corner of her eye she saw movement as the swinging door moved toward the living room but never made it back into the kitchen. Fingertips held it in place and then she saw a brown eye peek around the edge.

Help is here! She hoped so anyway. Who was it? Greg had blue eyes. It didn't matter. As long as they did something quickly so Margaret didn't die.

"Keep your hands where I can see them. Now move. And remember, I won't mind shooting you. I just don't want to. I want to clean this up quickly so they'll arrest you for Ken's murder." Dorothy took another step toward her.

"Police! Freeze!" a voice shouted.

The door from the hall and the door from the living room slammed open at the same time. Sam spun around on her heel, but Dorothy didn't freeze. She lifted the gun higher, pointing it straight at Sam. She saw Dorothy's finger start to squeeze the trigger. Just as quickly, Greg knocked the woman to the ground, and the gun flew from her hand, skidding across the floor.

The detective moved quickly and picked up the gun. Using his cell, he called for backup.

Greg flipped the woman facedown and jammed her hands behind her back. "Cuff her, Mark. She is your killer." Looking around, he said, "Sam, are you okay?"

Sam rushed past him, close to the swinging door. There, crumpled on the floor, was Margaret. "Quick, Greg. Call 911. Margaret's been shot!"

Greg pushed himself up on his feet as Dorothy hollered out in pain, "Watch it, mister. That hurts."

"You're lucky I don't kill you myself. Margaret better be all right, or you'll wish I had." He pulled out his cell and punched in 911. As he gave instructions over the phone, Mark took control of the prisoner, placing her in cuffs, and Greg moved over to Margaret's side.

Sam had her cradled in her lap, holding her head, whispering to her, trying to wake her. "You'll be okay, Margaret. Help is here. Greg is here. He's not going to let anything happen to you."

Her eyelashes started to flutter. "What . . . what happened?" she asked as Margaret started coming to her senses.

"It's over. Everything is over. Right, Greg?"

Laying his hand gently on Margaret's cheek, he smiled down at her. Lifting his gaze, he looked Sam in the eyes and said, "Yes. Now we all can start living again."

"For sure," Sam said, knowing Greg was speaking not only of Sam and her family, but he was including his plans for a future for him and Margaret.

Sam couldn't wait to be the one who told Marty.

EPILOGUE

Sam stood, staring out of the big picture window. After a month of red tape and various things, all was right with the world again, at least her little world, as the rain dribbled from the sky, dropping rhythmically across the lake, causing a steady pitter-patter. She took in a deep breath and then released it slowly. She had been thinking on her future and her life for the past several hours. Thoughts she couldn't believe she was thinking but thoughts that had great potential for her and Marty. Was it okay to be thinking about her future when people she'd known for a long time were in such horrid times in their own lives?

Dorothy Richardson was in prison waiting to stand trial for her husband's murder. Sam's heart broke for the woman . . . and her children. How would they survive?

Help me, Lord, to be all that You called me to be. Help me be the mother You'd want me to be. Help those three girls forgive their mother for what she has done, and most of all, help Dorothy to forgive herself as well as her husband in her heart so she can heal from this awful situation. Thank You for clearing my name and allowing my innocence to be made known. Help me be a testimony to You.

As Sam finished her prayer, she knew that a new day was upon them.

"Can I interrupt?" Greg said as he joined her in the living room.

"Be my guest. I'd love the company."

"I want your advice. Now that you've been cleared of all suspicions, I wanted to get to know Margaret a little better. I think I want what you and Matthew had, and I believe I could have that with her. She has taken me by surprise. I truly never thought I would fall in love, but when I'm around her, my heart perks up. In fact, I feel like a schoolboy around her. Do you think I'm too old to have these thoughts? Do you think it would be all right for me to pursue her?"

"I think I'm the wrong one to ask, but since you did ask, I'm going to say — go for it! I think you and Margaret will make a dynamite pair. I love you both. And you have my blessing."

The swinging door opened and Margaret stepped in, holding the door with one hand.

The yellow and purple shades of coloring to the left of her eye had almost faded completely away while the scar was still prominent from the flesh wound she'd received when shot at by Dorothy. Thank God it was nothing more serious and the woman was a lousy shot. Had Margaret not hit her head when falling down, she would have witnessed the whole incident . . . including Greg coming to her rescue. "Would either of you care for a cup of coffee?"

"Now's as good a time as any." Sam nudged Greg toward the door.

Margaret's eyes jumped from one to the other as she said, "What are you talking about?"

"Ugh. I was, ah, talking to Samantha about possibly taking you out to dinner . . . just you and me. Maybe even dinner and a movie," Greg said as he edged his way over to the door.

About that time, Marty came running into the room from the hallway looking for the remote. Picking it up, he stopped for a moment. Turning toward Greg, he said, "What about me? Can I come to the movies with you two?"

"Marty!" Sam started to correct him, but Greg cut her off.

"It's okay," he said holding his hand out toward Samantha as if saying wait a minute. Turning to Marty, he said, "Not this time, little buddy. I want to take Margaret out on a date." He grinned at the boy, exposing his teeth, and lifted his brows like Groucho. "Is that okay with you, Marty?"

"Boy-o-boy. You two on a date? Like Mom and Matthew did? Way cool! Isn't it, Momma?"

Greg shrugged. "It all depends on what Margaret says. I think we have something there. And at this time in my life I don't want to mess around . . . I'm not looking for a good time."

"You hurt my feelings," Margaret said as she punched Greg in the arm. "If you don't think we'll have a good time, then why are you asking me out?"

"You get me wrong, dear," he said as he took her by the hand. "I know we'll have a good time wherever we go and whatever we do — but if what I'm feeling is the real thing, like I think it is, I want us to have a good time . . . for the rest of our lives. You and me. Do you know what I mean? I mean, at our stage in life, if this is love I'm feeling and you find you feel the same way, I don't want to play around. I want us to get married and live together . . . forever."

Margaret's eyes widened as Sam's mouth dropped.

"Am I rushing things a bit?" Greg questioned, looking from one to the other, holding his hands up in the air. "Sorry."

Margaret's eyes brightened, and a smile illuminated her face. She shook her head. "I know exactly what you mean, and I'm with you 100 percent."

Greg matched Margaret's grin as he opened his arms. Margaret slipped right in. Closing his arms around her, he lowered his face, closing the distance between them, and pressed his lips to hers for a brief moment. Then he whispered, "What a perfect fit!"

Marty squealed with excitement.

Quickly Sam covered his mouth, trying to stifle his exuberance, not wanting to disturb the couple. He shook his head back and forth until he freed himself from his mom's hold. "Oh, Momma, does that mean Greg is going to live here, too? Oh, boy." The little boy was jumping up and down, unable to hide his joy.

Overhearing the dear boy's question, they both started to laugh. Greg, not letting loose of Margaret with his right arm wrapped around her waist, turned toward Marty. "Sorry, little buddy, but when we marry, I'll bring Margaret home to live with me, if she'll have me."

Marty's smile faded quickly.

"But don't think you're going to lose us. I hope you'll think of us as grandparents. We're family . . . and don't you forget it."

"Oh, Greg. How sweet. Thank you." Sam's heart felt like it was about to explode.

Sam and Marty rushed to the couple's side, and the four fell into a group hug as tears streamed down Margaret's face — tears of joy.

While the four embraced, Sam wondered. *Is now the time? It's perfect timing.* As Sam broke free, she said, "While we're making plans for your future, I have something I want to throw in the pot, but I think we have to talk about this sitting down."

"You're looking serious, Sam. Should I go make a pot of coffee now?"

"Thanks, Margaret, but no. I think the four of us should sit down right here in the living room while I share some thoughts that have come to me in the past few hours."

Greg slid his arm from Margaret's waist and caught her by the hand. "I like this. Our first family meeting." A smile spread across his face as he tugged Margaret's hand and led her to the sofa. They sat close, holding one another's hand.

Sam, slipping into Matthew's chair, said,

316

"Marty, you grab a seat. This includes you, too."

"Oh boy, oh boy." He jumped on the other end of the sofa. "I'm all ears."

Greg stole a peck on Margaret's cheek, and then said, "You've got my full attention, Samantha. What's up?"

"During the time I was a suspect in the death of Ken Richardson, I was forced to wonder if that was the end of my life as a mother, as a friend, and as a dispatcher. I started thinking, I know God's got a special plan for me, and I don't think it is working at the trucking company anymore." Glancing at each of their faces, she said, "You know how I say everything happens for a reason?"

Greg and Margaret nodded in unison as Marty said, "Yes, Mom. We know. That's your answer to everything that goes wrong."

For a brief moment, laughter filled the air.

When everything settled, Samantha continued, "Well, I truly believe it. I believe it so much that it hit me a few hours ago: the serial killer, my time with Matthew, and now this ordeal, what has come from it? What purpose did it serve? For what reason did all of this happen? Then it hit me, we may not have Matthew anymore, but he set us up for life. I don't have to work to support us. He did that. We have enough money to take care of us, so I think it's time I, we, take care of others."

Greg frowned as he glanced at Margaret and then to Sam. "What do you mean? You're going to start taking people in and take care of them? We're not married yet, and you really don't have that much room."

"Don't be silly. I'm going to have to learn how to take care of Marty and I now that you're stealing away our lovely caretaker, friend, and grandmother." She laughed as she spoke. "With our blessings, I might add."

"I'm glad to hear that." Margaret flashed Sam a smile of love.

"But seriously. I think God has shown me other people go through situations that put their lives in jeopardy and get accused of things they didn't do, but aren't as lucky as me to have dear friends who know the ropes, know the law, know how to help them. I'm quitting the trucking company and, if you're game," she said pointing to Greg and to Margaret, "I'd like us to start our own business, trying to help others. You know, like a private investigator service. You being the head PI, of course. You are retired, you know, even though you keep working. And I will train and learn and get a license, but in the meantime, I can do some things to help."

Greg squeezed Margaret's hand. Looking at this woman, as love seemed to be pouring out of his eyes, he said, "I was going to tell you, Margaret, I plan to resign my job as bodyguard to the Governor. I've only worked all this time because I had no life — no one I cared to be with. I have a monthly pension that would more than take care of us, as well as a great deal of savings. I mean it's not like I owe on my house or have any bills. So since I haven't been spending, it's been piling up. Now I am hoping to enjoy the rest of my life with you."

Turning his eyes on Sam, he added, "So I am free to start working on the side . . . if Margaret agrees. But mind you, I don't want to work all the time. I want my honey and me to do a little traveling and just plain enjoy life while enjoying one another. So if she agrees, and God is behind everything, you can count me in."

"Me, too! I think you both have grand notions, and I'm ready for both. I've always wanted to travel. And in case you didn't know it, Sam, I didn't take this job Matthew offered me because I was in need of money. My husband left me quite well-off, too. So it sounds like money won't be a problem to get your new business off the ground." She laughed as she reached around Greg, hugging him. "I can't believe we're about to start living at our age."

"You and me both," Greg whispered. "I never thought I'd find true love. And look what I've got — love, family, and a new life. Wow!"

If Sam didn't know better, she believed she saw tears materializing on the rims of Greg's eyelids. Was he about to cry? She knew she was on the verge of tears.

Sam jumped to her feet and rushed over to the happy couple. Wrapping her arms around them both, she said, "Thank you so much. It just feels so right, doesn't it?"

Before they could answer, Marty, with arms spread and a puzzled look on his face, said "What about me? Where do I fit in?" He had sat quietly listening to all the adults through this whole ordeal, but now he seemed to feel left out.

Samantha rushed to her son's side and knelt down before him as he was still seated on the couch. "Sweetheart, you are in all of this! My question to you is, will you be able to handle having your mom home almost every day? And I'll be cooking, or should I say fixing you something to èat — I'm still not the best cook in the world. Margaret can teach me if she will. But I'll be fixing all of your meals. Can you handle a momma 24-7?"

This time Marty was the one jumping up off the sofa. "All right, Momma." He wrapped his arms around her neck, as she was still down on her knees by the couch. "This sounds great! Count me in, too!"

ABOUT THE AUTHOR

Deborah Lynne, beloved inspirational romance, mystery, and romance-suspense writer, has penned eight novels: *After You're Gone, Crime in the Big Easy,* The Samantha Cain Mysteries *(Be Not Afraid, Testimony of Innocence, The Truth Revealed), Grace: A Gift of Love, All in God's Time,* and *Passion from the Heart.*

She is an active member of ACFW, RWA, and HEARTLA. She enjoys sharing her stories with her readers as well as the knowledge she gains as she grows as a novelist with other writers who share the same dream — of becoming a published author. She and her family enjoy their relaxed life in Louisiana.

http://www.author-deborahlynne.com
www.oaktara.com

The employees of Thorndike Press hope you have enjoyed this Large Print book. All our Thorndike, Wheeler, and Kennebec Large Print titles are designed for easy reading, and all our books are made to last. Other Thorndike Press Large Print books are available at your library, through selected bookstores, or directly from us.

For information about titles, please call:
  (800) 223-1244

or visit our Web site at:
  http://gale.cengage.com/thorndike

To share your comments, please write:
  Publisher
  Thorndike Press
  10 Water St., Suite 310
  Waterville, ME 04901